THE DARKEST MAGIC

RITE WORLD: VAMPIRE WARS BOOK 3

JULIANA HAYGERT

AUTHOR'S NOTE

I hope you enjoy reading *The Darkest Magic*!

Don't forget to sign up for my Newsletter to find out about new releases, cover reveals, giveaways, and more!

If you want to see exclusive teasers, help me decide on covers, read excerpts, talk about books, etc, join my reader group on Facebook: Juliana's Club!

Welcome to the RITE WORLD!

Free Novella:
The Vampire Hunt

Novellas:
The Hunter Path
The Light Calling
The Light Witch
The Wicked Alliance

Rite World:
The Vampire Heir (Book 1)
The Witch Queen (Book 2)
The Immortal Vow (Book 3)
The Warlock Lord (Book 4)
The Wolf Consort (Book 5)
The Crystal Rose (Book 6)
The Wolf Forsaken (Book 7)
The Fae Bound (Book 8)
The Blood Pact (Book 9)

Rite World: Blackthorn Hunters Academy
The Demons Kiss (Book 1)
The Hunter Secret (Book 2)
The Soul Bond (Book 3)
The Shadow Trials (Book 4)
The Immortal Vow (Book 5)

Rite World: Lightgrove Witches
The Midnight Test (Book 1)
The Midnight Spell (Book 2)
The Midnight Flame (Book 3)

Rite World: Vampire Wars
The Darkest Vampire (Book 1)
The Darkest Witch (Book 2)
The Darkest Magic (Book 3)

Rite World: Night Wolves
The Night Calling (Book 1)

And more to come!

THE VAMPIRE HUNT

I have an exclusive novella set in the Rite World that is just for my newsletter subscribers!
Click here to sign-up and receive your book!

THE VAMPIRE HUNT
A Rite World Novella

Norah is a demon hunter, one of the best graduated from the Blackthorn Hunters Academy. When she's sent to investigate a case concerning demons in a small town, she runs into a very arrogant vampire. Her first instinct is to kill him, after all, he's a supernatural and demon hunters are taught to end all evil.

Cain is a vampire prince. Because of his status, he's in charge of making sure humans don't find out about his kind. During a routine investigation, he bumps into a very sexy demon hunter and he wonders what she's doing on his way.

However, the case grows much bigger for Norah and Cain to handle alone. To find the truth and win this battle, the vampire and the demon hunter will have to hunt together—without killing each other.

How well could this end?

1

LAVINIA

This was worse than a nightmare.

The bedroom Tack had taken me to wasn't as big and fancy as the one I had had at the Nightmist coven or at DuMoir Castle, but it was still bigger than my old bedroom in Forest Creek. It reminded of a hotel room—a longish entrance hall with a built-in closet and door to a bathroom, then a rectangular space with a queen bed with white bedding, two nightstands flanking the bed, paintings of random landscapes decorating the walls, a dresser with mirror lining the wall opposite the bed, and an armchair in the corner by the window.

My first instinct once I was left alone was to race to the window for two things: to find out where I was and to check if I could scale down it.

When I pulled back the heavy curtains, bright light greeted me. It was probably the middle of the day, though I couldn't see the sun from here.

I was on the second floor and tall trees surrounded the building. We were in the middle of a forest? I didn't know why, but I thought the warlocks would be hiding in a cave or something equally dark, evil, and creepy.

I couldn't see much from the building. However, the windowsill was made of long, thick logs. After unlatching the window, I shoved against the edge; it didn't budge. I had been expecting that. I snatched the metal lamp from the night-stand, yanking the plug from the wall outlet, and threw it at the window.

The lamp thumped against the glass with a crystalline sound. Lamp and shattered light bulb fell on the carpeted floor. The window remained intact—not even a crack. With a roar of frustration, I snatched the lamp from the floor and smashed it against the window repeatedly.

Nothing happened.

Panting for breath, I stared at the damn window. Was it enchanted?

I called my magic, throwing a bolt at the center of the pane. It ricocheted off the glass. With a shriek of surprise, I ducked, covering my head with my arms as the bolt rico-cheted off the walls, ceiling, and floor, and finally fizzled out when it struck one of the paintings, knocking it off the wall.

Shit.

Burn marks on the walls scorched the places the bolt had hit, but the damn window wouldn't break.

A knock came from the door. I heard the click as someone unlocked it and pushed it open. Tack came in, holding a wooden tray with food.

He looked at the walls, the lamp and the painting on the floor. "The room is warded. You can't break the window or open it. Don't waste your time trying." He placed the tray on the dresser. "Now, eat, witch. You'll need your strength later."

I opened my mouth but closed it again. What would I

say? Insult him? Demand he let me go? Cry that I wouldn't eat? I held no power in this situation.

Without another glance at me, Tack walked away, the lock slipping into place behind him.

A heavy feeling settled in my chest, my shoulders sagging in defeat.

Despair crept over me in a wave, choking me with sadness and frustration. The warlocks had kidnapped me; I was locked in a warded room without any chance of escaping.

And Killian was at DuMoir Castle.

How long had it been since I was taken? Had he noticed my absence? Would he come for me?

Tears brimmed in my eyes.

Killian wouldn't know where to look, and everyone had assumed for twenty years that he had been killed or left. Would he believe the same? That I had left him?

I couldn't sit here, waiting for a miracle.

I wiped the tears from my eyes and inhaled deeply.

I *would* escape from here.

<hr>

My best chance of escape was to go with the flow for now to learn everything about this place and the warlocks' habits.

I nibbled on the sandwich and drank the juice that had been brought to me. I found clean sweatpants, leggings, sweaters, jackets, and dresses in the closet—all black or dark gray, and not exactly my size. I took a quick shower and put on leggings with a long sweatshirt.

Then I waited.

Bates unlocked my door, but he didn't come in. "Follow me," was all he said.

I pretended to be a little reluctant but followed him out of the bedroom. As we walked through the hallway, I noticed the place looked like a mansion. A wide hallway with doors lining the dark walls, and at the end, an L-shaped staircase. We went down, but I saw there was another flight going up. So there were at least three levels to this house. The staircase opened into a large foyer and just beyond it, a living area furnished with couches, rugs, a fireplace, and a TV.

Bates gestured for me to follow him into a side hallway. This one had only three doors. One door was open—a half bath. The other two doors were closed. Bates opened one and jerked his head.

I stepped through and halted.

In a normal house, this would have been a spare guest room or an office, but it was a vast room with dark walls, stone floors, and a high ceiling.

A large white circle with fifteen points was drawn on the floor in the center of the room. Two of those points were occupied by black boxes.

I felt the blood rushing from my face.

Were these Killian's and Twyla's boxes? Had they stolen the boxes when they kidnapped me? I didn't feel a pull toward them.

"Are those ...?" I couldn't say it.

Just outside the circle, Eldon, Tack, and Damien heard me. They stopped talking among themselves and turned to me.

"The boxes you found and gave to the vampires?" Eldon asked, his voice hard. "No. We couldn't get those boxes ... yet."

I didn't know if that was a good or a bad answer. Because then it meant ... "You've found two other boxes."

Damien nodded. "Pretty and clever. A rare combo."

A whip of rage slashed through me. I held on to it with both hands, even as it burned my skin. In here, it would be better to feed my rage and anger than to let my fear show.

Eldon's brow furrowed. "I heard you tried to break out of your bedroom by breaking the window. I thought I told you there's no way to escape this place."

That was what they wanted me to believe. Nothing was impossible. I had to play this right.

"You didn't think I would just accept my fate," I said.

Eldon looked amused with my answer. "Truth be told, no, but the sooner you do, the less unpleasant your stay here will be."

The sooner I accepted my fate, or pretended to, the sooner I would be able to find a way out of here.

I had to. I wasn't naive. I knew what they wanted with me. Why I was here.

My gaze shifted to the boxes in the circle.

Eldon followed my line of sight. "Are you ready to comply, witch?"

I swallowed. He wanted me to open the boxes. "What if I refuse?"

The warlock rolled his eyes. "Must we go through this again? You'll only make things more difficult, and painful, for yourself."

Shit. But opening those boxes? Well, perhaps if they had supernaturals inside like Killian and Twyla, then I could ask for help. We could flee this place. We had done something similar with the Nightmist coven.

I frowned. If I agreed immediately, they would know I

was up to something. Taking a step back, I shook my head. "I won't do it."

Bates stepped closer to me, Tack moved around the circle, and Damien gave me a predatory grin.

"Who says we're giving you a choice?" Eldon asked.

I turned to leave the room, but Bates stood in my way. A second later, Tack had his hand around my upper arm. I threw my weight back while they dragged me to the center of the circle.

Tack and Bates held my arms, keeping me upright, and Damien stood behind me, in case I tried to run again. Eldon picked up a box as they brought me forward. His lips curled in a wicked grin as he extended the box to me.

I stared at it and a spark of apprehension flickered through me. What if the box contained a wolf shifter and it pounced on me and ripped my throat before I could say anything?

This time, when Tack moved his hand to my wrist and pulled my arm straight in front of me, I did resist for real.

Eldon pushed the box into my hand.

My fingers brushed against the smooth stone, and instantly, the box changed. Ridges appeared on its surface, and a bright light came from them. The box shook and Eldon dropped it. It opened and smoke came out.

We all stepped back.

The smoke dissipated ... and there was no one.

"It's one of the empty boxes," I muttered, stunned. I knew there were more empty boxes out there than ones serving as a prison for supernaturals, but I didn't really consider them until now.

Eldon groaned. "It's okay. We have another one here." He picked up the next box and offered it to me.

This time, Tack didn't have to force my hand forward. A slight tug did the trick. I reached for it, taking the box from Eldon. The ridges and light appeared. The box shook so hard, I dropped it. It fell to the floor and opened, smoke rising from within.

And once more, no one came from inside.

I didn't know if I should sigh in relief or shock.

Eldon cursed under his breath. "Empty boxes."

"They won't be empty for long," Tack said. He and Bates had let me go but hadn't moved away. "I heard from Chess. They located an angel and a goblin."

I stared at him. They hadn't only gotten me and were after the boxes. They were also securing more supernaturals to fill the empty boxes. Even though I had known about their plan, my brain was still putting two and two together.

Instead of dread for what was to come, I felt a little giddy. A small grin adorned my lips.

Tack glared at me. "What are you smiling about?"

"Because you only have two boxes. Two others are practically unattainable, and the remaining eleven are lost."

"Not for long." Eldon walked to a long, narrow counter on the side of the room. From among loose pages, quills, ink, and some empty vials, he picked up another box, smaller and squarer. "The prototype. The first box Soren and Acalla made when creating the spell. It can track the other boxes." He tilted his head, his eyes on me. "That's how we found you and your boxes."

"That's how we found these two." Damien gestured to the floor.

"And that's how we'll find all of them," Tack said.

Oh, shit.

I HAD TOLD myself I would stay and do what they wanted, for now, but I still couldn't sit in my bedroom and wait. My brain kept coming up with ideas of how to escape. Their plan was more advanced than I expected. They had me. They had two other boxes, were securing supernaturals to put into them, and had a way of locating more boxes.

I needed to find a way to stop them.

I dressed in thick leggings, a dark sweater, and boots. I tied my hair in a ponytail. I halted before the locked door and rolled my shoulders. I closed my eyes and focused, calling my magic. Now that my aunt had broken the blood promise, an avalanche of power answered, filling my veins, pushing against my skin, asking for release. I gritted my teeth, trying to control it. I didn't have experience with this much power, but if I exploded in a ball of magic right now, I didn't care, as long as it helped me get out of here.

In my mind, I visualized the lock and poured my magic into it. I imagined myself using a key and unlocking the door. A click sounded and I opened my eyes. Had it worked? Apprehensive, I reached for the door and turned the knob.

The door opened.

I wanted to cheer, but pressed my lips tight and contained my excitement. I would celebrate once I was away from here, safe and sound.

I would celebrate once I was back with Killian.

Killian ...

My heart squeezed. He was probably going crazy right now. After losing his parents, his sister, and then his brother, losing me must be the blow that either brought him to his knees, or pushed him over the edge.

I shook my head and pushed thoughts of Killian from my mind. Getting distracted with my distress and longing would only make things harder.

I tiptoed out of my bedroom and glanced side to side. The corridor was empty and quiet. Had all the warlocks gone to bed?

I made my way through the corridor toward the staircase, descending to the front door.

It was way too easy.

It should have made me worried, but I didn't dare over-think this.

Unfortunately, I couldn't just leave. I turned right before the front door and took the hallway that led to the room where the warlocks had shown me the boxes, what I was calling the summoning room in my head.

Holding my breath, I entered the room. A thin strip of moonlight came from a rectangular window near the ceiling. The darkness gave me pause, but I steeled myself and pushed through my fear. Once more, I told myself: anger over fear. So I held on to anger and stepped farther into the room. The boxes were in the same place, in their corners of the large circle. And the prototype was on the narrow table along the sidewall.

Walking around the circle, I went to the table. I fished the small hand towel I had grabbed from my bathroom, wrapped it around the box, and picked it up in my arms. I didn't know if the prototype would react to my touch the same way as the others did, but I wouldn't take risks.

I started for the door, then paused. I glanced at the two empty boxes. No, I didn't need to take those too. They were empty and without me, the warlocks wouldn't be able to lock supernaturals inside them.

I only needed to take the prototype, since they used it to track the other boxes. That was what I wanted to stop.

With the box secured in my arms, I tiptoed to the door.

It closed with a resounding click. I gasped and stepped back, my heart hammering in my chest.

Four figures emerged from the corners of the rooms.

What the ...

Eldon, Tack, Damien, and Bates stalked toward me, their eyes shining dark in the dim light.

"Now, what do we have here?" Eldon asked. The overhead lights turned on and I had to close my eyes for a moment. "A witch trying to steal the boxes and escape? Who would have thought of that?"

I hugged the box and fumed at him, once more choosing anger over fear. "What did you think I would do? Sit and smile?"

Eldon let out a hollow laugh. "We're here, aren't we?"

I bristled. Damn it. I had been so close. If only I had left the prototype behind, I could have already been half a mile away. No, there was no way I could leave without it.

I would have to find another way.

Tack extended his hand to me. "Give me the box, witch."

I hugged the box tighter. "Make me."

Eldon's lips peeled back. "With pleasure." He twisted his hand.

Pain started deep in my gut and spread through my veins. I gasped and fell to my knees. The box rolled from my arms as I pressed a hand over my stomach. Eldon moved his hands and the pain flared up. Fire licked my insides, boiling my blood, melting my organs, frying my brain. I curled on the floor in front of them, but all I could think about was the pain.

A few seconds later, Eldon lowered his hand.

The pain subsided, but didn't go away, at least not yet. I inhaled deeply, trying to calm my racing heart, my shaking limbs.

Tack picked up the prototype box and walked away with it.

Eldon crouched down beside me. "Remember this, witch. The potion that runs through your veins prevents you from using your magic against us? It also allows me to control you. To hurt you."

Enraged tears brimmed in my eyes. So, even if I was able to run, Eldon could flick his hands and inflict pain, making it impossible for me to move.

Great.

"Like I said before," he continued, his wicked smile still splitting his face. "You have no way out of here."

2

KILLIAN

I PACED IN FRONT OF DRAKE'S DESK.

It had been two days since Lavinia was kidnapped. DuMoir Castle was still in lockdown, every inch of the castle had been searched, and everyone in here had been fully questioned. Shane, the werewolf we had freed when fleeing from the Nightmist witches, had helped me search the grounds outside, but there was no track, no clue, no scent, nothing. It was like Lavinia had vanished into thin air.

"Someone must know something," I said through gritted teeth. It had been hard to hide my anger and frustration. Honestly, most of the time, I didn't bother trying to.

"Killian, we've been over this." Seated in his chair, Drake let out a long sigh. He was tired of me; I knew that. I was tired of myself, of this situation. I had to do something!

I halted, glaring at him. "Then we question everyone again!"

His green eyes remained impassive. "I understand your feelings, believe me. Thea and I have been through a lot together, and whenever she was hurt or in trouble, I would have done anything for her. Even lose reason."

"Don't," I snarled.

"I'm here as the reason. We will find Lavinia, we will bring her back, but fighting with everyone in the castle won't solve anything."

I crossed my arms. "I'm not fighting."

Drake snorted. "That's your perspective. Everyone else thinks you've lost it and you're a second away from ripping everyone's throat."

I groaned. My shoulders sagged and I plopped down on a leather chair across the glass desk. "I can't sit here and wait. What about if Thea made a truth serum? We could give it to everyone in the castle before we question them again."

"As much as I think that idea has merit, I'm trying to be a fair leader," Drake said. "I won't force anyone to take the truth serum."

"Then don't force them. Just offer it to them. If they refuse, then we know they have something to hide."

"Some people don't want to share anything about themselves, Killian. Some might not want to take it because they don't want us to know some stupid, meaningless things about themselves." He paused. "But ... your idea has merit. I'll consider it."

I let out a long breath. Consider it. That could take an hour, or a month. "Meanwhile, Lavinia is suffering at the hands of the warlocks."

"One, we don't know it was really this group of warlocks who took her." I opened my mouth to protest, but he continued, "But I agree, it makes the most sense. Two, if she's the only one besides Almae who can open the boxes and manipulate their magic, then they won't hurt her. They won't risk it."

I gritted my teeth and clenched my fists. I knew he was right, but I stopped the anger from rising again. Even if the warlocks didn't hurt her, she was there alone among them, and they could be scaring her, treating her like a slave ... or worse.

I didn't know how long I could stand this.

A knock came from the door a second before it opened and Cain walked inside. "We're here, my lord." He opened the door wider and the other princes walked in—Dorian, Aston, Gray, and Patrick.

My gut tightened every time I looked at Patrick. The bastard had become prince almost twenty years ago, right after I disappeared. I could only guess that I would have turned prince before him had I not been kidnapped by Soren's warlocks.

Now, he was in the lead.

Lord Drake ended up crowning me prince without the ceremony on the night Lavinia disappeared. He said an event to celebrate that felt wrong but having me as a prince would facilitate things while we solved this mystery, and I agreed. So I accepted the title without any pomp.

Cain sat in the chair beside me, while the other three princes stood behind us. I had asked Drake on our first night back, before Lavinia disappeared, why he hadn't filled out the other princes' spots. He told me that Reynard hadn't come up with ten. It had just happened. Drake hoped in the future to nominate more princes, but he said he had to feel they deserve it, not just because they wanted more numbers.

It made sense.

"Report," Drake said.

"My contacts haven't seen or heard anything," Cain said.

The others nodded in agreement.

"I find it hard to believe a powerful group of warlocks has been hiding right under our noses," Drake mused. "I talked to Keeran last night. He assured me these are not his warlocks, but he also mentioned that many warlocks went missing after he defeated Soren."

I frowned. Soren, who wasn't dead. No, he was living in Unity, a hidden town founded by Almae, but he wasn't himself. He was like an empty shell. That was the only reason Keeran hadn't killed him. Because it would have been soulless of him to kill someone, his own father, who couldn't defend himself.

I could see the logic in that, but right now, it was hard to agree with it. All in all, I thought the world would be a better place with Soren truly gone.

"I saw Tack with these warlocks," I told them. "He was there when I was being held by Soren."

Drake nodded. "Keeran met all of Soren's warlocks a few years back, so he's coming to help. We're still in lockdown, but we'll open the gates so he and Luana can enter."

Luana was the alpha of a magical kind of werewolves, and Keeran's mate.

So many things had changed ...

"One thing is for sure," Aston spoke up. "It seems these warlocks are looking to finish the spell Soren started twenty years ago."

"Which means, they will need the boxes we have," Gray added.

"The boxes are secured," Dorian said.

"Right," Drake agreed. "They won't be able to go through

all of us to get to them. Besides, I'll talk to Keeran about lending us some of his warlocks to help out here."

More warlocks. I wasn't sure I liked this idea, though we needed to ensure no one got the boxes. If we had to surround the castle with an army, so be it.

"Still, we should try to stop them," Patrick said.

Hearing his voice grated on my nerves. I thought twenty years could change that, but apparently it hadn't.

"We'll get Lavinia back." I glanced at Patrick. "And when we do, we'll kill them all."

"Of course," he said, one corner of his lips curling up.

I shot to my feet. "What are you smiling about?"

Instantly, he was serious again. "Smiling? You must be seeing things."

I walked up to him, ready to punch his pretty face. "You think this is funny, don't you?"

"Killian, you're losing your mind," he said. "Have you fed since your mate was taken? Have you slept?"

"Don't change the subject, Patrick," I snarled.

He faced me, his eyes hard. "I'm not, asshat."

"Prince Killian, Prince Patrick." Drake rose from his chair, his voice cold and unyielding. "This is not the time for rivalries." He locked his eyes on me. "I hate to say this, Killian, but he's right. You have to feed and sleep. Being weak and irritable won't do you any good."

I opened my mouth to protest but closed it again. I wasn't a teenager. Instead, I turned toward the door. I glanced at Patrick as I walked past him, and sure enough, he had that same half-grin adorning his lips.

It took everything in me not to turn around and punch that grin right off his face.

I marched out of Drake's office. Lewis and Holden, two

vampires who had been under Drake's wings, stood by the door as guards. They seemed loyal ... anyone in this castle looked loyal. And yet, someone had taken Lavinia.

My rage spiked again and I pivoted, punching the nearest wall. The stone cracked under my fists and pain jolted through my arm. I glanced at my hand and the bloodied knuckles ... this felt good. It felt like a release. I needed to punch more things. More people. Maybe I could do that on a cocky vampire who liked to antagonize me.

I shook my head. No, I couldn't let Patrick get to me. Lavinia deserved the best from me, and that meant I had to rein in my emotions to make the right decisions.

Exhaling, I went up the stairs. I turned toward the guest wing and almost bumped into Shane ,which was ridiculous, since I should have heard him coming. I was so off my game ...

"Hey," Shane called out. "Dude, you look like shit. When was the last time you slept?"

I groaned. Why was suddenly everyone asking me that? Truth be told, I hadn't slept or fed since learning what happened to Lavinia. "What does it matter?" I barked.

Shane lifted his hands. "I'm just asking."

"Sorry." I rolled my shoulders. "I'm just tense."

"I bet." The wolf shifter pressed his lips tight. "You want to go out and search the grounds again? Maybe we missed something."

Though I liked the idea of having something to do, I knew it was useless. We had scoured the damn forest around the castle. Going out now wouldn't magicked a new clue.

During the past two days, Shane had been a fixture around the castle. He didn't mingle much with the vampires, but he helped out whenever he could. And he seemed to be worried about Lavinia too.

"She helped free me," he had said when I asked why he had volunteered to search the grounds with me. "I owe her. Besides, as a wolf shifter, I have a surprisingly good nose."

Despite everything, his wit and insufferable charm grew a little each day. I couldn't imagine what he had had been like with his pack, because Shane was confident. I probably wouldn't have been able to swallow being around him.

Life had a way of remaking us all—even Twyla.

Twyla was a shadow fae who had been trapped in the box we recovered from the Nightmist coven in central Canada. She had been taken by Soren and his crew and put inside her box a couple of months before me. Since arriving at DuMoir Castle, she had barely left her bedroom. Almae had asked to see her, but Twyla still had the picture of Almae—Acalla— helping Soren. I had always known Almae hadn't done it of her own free will.

"Not right now," I told Shane. "I should take Drake's advice to feed and rest. After that, we can see if they came up with another idea and we can make ourselves useful."

"Sounds like a plan." Shane placed a heavy hand on my shoulder. "Hang in there, man. She'll be fine."

I nodded. I truly hoped that was true.

Shane went on his way and I walked to Lavinia's bedroom. Two nights ago, we had made love. I had told her I loved her, and she had told me she loved me. The mating bond had snapped and our lives had joined.

And then she was snatched from under my nose.

I opened the door and walked in.

As I expected, Almae was still here. She had been here since Lavinia was taken. Kneeling on the stone floor, with blessed chalk, herbs, and potions around her, Almae cast spells to track Lavinia. Even Lavinia's cracked phone, the only clue we found, was beside her. At some point, she even created her own spells and potions.

But nothing worked.

She saw me standing outside the large circle she had drawn on the floor. She paused for a breath, then continued chanting in a language I didn't recognize. The woman would kill herself like this.

For that alone, I could almost forgive her for what she had done to me.

"Almae," I called. She ignored me as she drew more symbols on the floor in a frantic state. "Almae, look at me."

"I can't," she whispered. "I can't stop now. I can feel it." She turned wide eyes at me. "I can feel the magic around her, blocking her from my reach. I have to break it. I need to. Once I do, I'll be able to see her. We'll find her."

"You won't find her if you're passed out."

"Hush." She sent a wave of magic at me, pushing me back several feet, until I was almost out the door. I moved as fast as my powers allowed me, grasped the doorjamb, and pushed myself back inside before she slammed the door with a resonating thud.

I didn't want to disrupt her. If anyone could break the blockage the warlocks had put around Lavinia, it was her. But if she fell ill, she wouldn't be able to continue this.

"Almae, Lavinia wouldn't want you to kill yourself to find her," I said, my tone hard.

She picked up some herbs from the floor and stood. "This is all my fault! All my fault!" She glanced around the floor. "I made those boxes, powered them. If Lavinia hadn't been related to me, she wouldn't be able to open them, and they wouldn't have been after her. They would have come to me instead." Her shoulders sagged. "It's all my fault."

"Almae," I repeated, but I didn't know what to say. I felt like it was my fault too. Not in the same way, but I was Lavinia's mate. I had sworn to protect her, to be with her, to make sure she was okay.

And yet, I had left her alone and she was kidnapped from my home.

When I got her back—and I *would* get her back—I would never leave her alone again.

I stepped into the circle, but the magic pushed me back. I couldn't cross it. "Shit," I muttered.

The door behind me opened, and Thea and Aurora walked in. Thea halted by my side and stared at the crazy witch in horror, while Aurora seemed unfazed by the sight.

"What in the name of the stars is going on?" she asked in a low voice.

"She'll collapse at this rate," I told her.

When I first met Thea a couple of days ago, I had been skeptical of her. A queen witch mated to the lord of DuMoir Castle? But Thea had surprised me. She had been kind and firm and level-headed while dealing with everything going on. I had heard stories of how she had practically saved Drake, and how he had saved her. Apparently, their bond went back eons.

"Someone has to make her stop, but I can't enter the circle."

Thea nodded.

Without missing a beat, the little girl waved her hand in front of her and a crackling of power shifted through the room. She gestured for her mother to proceed.

As stunned as I was, Thea stepped into the circle and walked to Almae.

She put her arm around Almae's shoulder. "My friend, come with me."

Almae turned to Thea with wild eyes, and then her expression slacked, her eyes softened, her chest deflated. Thea was using magic to calm Almae. The older witch nodded, and when Thea tugged her forward, she let Thea guide her out of the circle. Aurora reached for the old witch's hand and held tight.

Thea gave me a sympathetic glance before walking out with Aurora and Almae.

I looked around the messy bedroom. The circle, the chalk, the herbs ... it was like a tornado had come through here.

Slowly, I made my way to the bed and sat on the soft mattress. I smoothed my hand over the bedsheets and inhaled deeply. Despite everything Almae had done, Lavinia's scent still hung heavy in the air—and in the bed. I lay down and hugged the pillow, letting her scent overwhelm my senses.

If I had to rest, I would at least pretend she was right beside me.

3

KILLIAN

Nightmares featuring Lavinia riddled my sleep. They were random sequences from my past merged with everyday things—like swimming in a lake, leaving a nightclub, or driving my old MacLaren. However, each subconscious story ended with her dead or gone, and me alone in the darkness.

Despite my agitated sleep, I felt better when I woke up later that evening. Now I just needed to go hunting and I would be ready to bring down the world in order to rescue Lavinia.

I felt defeated and hopeless as I went to my bedroom. My room wasn't the same from twenty years ago. Back then, I was one more soldier in Lord Reynard's army and my room had been located with the other soldiers in the common wing of the castle. Lord Drake had given me one of the large chambers in the royal wing, near his own.

I walked in the double doors and stopped. I had agreed to become a prince, something I had coveted my entire life, because it would give me the authority I needed to search for Lavinia, to command other vampires to help me. However, my chambers in the castle felt empty and wrong, as if I was in this for the opulence and status. Once, I had cared about those things. Now, I would sleep in the stables with the horses if it meant having Lavinia back.

With a sigh, I crossed the sitting area, the bedroom, and disappeared into my bathroom where I took a long shower.

That helped me relax, although I honestly wouldn't relax completely until I had Lavinia here with me. In my walk-in closet, I found a black suit, black shirt, and black shoes—they matched my mood.

I was buttoning the shirt in front of the floor-length mirror when someone knocked on the door. Frowning, I went to it and opened it wide.

"My prince," said Elder, one of Cain's men. He had been a lower-ranked vampire when I lived here long ago, but he had already been working for Cain. We had gone on several missions together. "Lord Drake requests your presence in the guests wing's sitting room. The warlock is here."

Instantly, I tensed.

I thanked Elder, exited into the hallway with him, closed the door behind me, and ran to the sitting room.

Thea and Almae sat on the claw-footed couch in the middle of the room, turned to the tall silver fireplace to the right, where a billowing fire raged. Aurora played on the thick rug before the couch, covering a good portion of the stone floors, and Drake stood by one of the long windows on the other side of the room, which opened to a balcony that overlooked the maze outside.

I halted beside Drake. "Where is he?"

"He arrived a few minutes ago and is being escorted here," Drake told me.

I nodded and glanced to Almae. "How is she?"

"Better. Thea gave her some tea and she slept most of the afternoon."

Good. I believed her magic could help us in finding Lavinia—after all, she had found us before—but she couldn't do that if she was exhausted.

Almae pointed her finger up, shooting a tiny pink firework at the ceiling. Aurora squealed with laughter. I had to admit, the little girl was fascinating. Besides looking like a porcelain doll with her green eyes and black curls, she was a rare half-witch, half-vampire, and destined to be the Queen of All Witches when she came of age. I hadn't seen much of her, but the few moments we had spent in the same room, she behaved mostly like a child, and then suddenly commented like she was a young adult. Or she performed spells way beyond her age, like when she broke into Almae's magical circle earlier today. Most mature witches couldn't have done that.

It was disconcerting.

Aurora threw her arms up in the air and a dozen fireworks of all colors exploded above her head. She laughed. Beside me, Drake smiled.

I frowned.

A moment later, the faint click of footsteps reached my ears. I looked at Drake and he nodded, having heard it too.

I straightened and braced myself. I didn't know what to expect. I was about to meet a warlock, the Warlock Lord who took over for Soren. Almae's and Soren's son, who could have answers.

Until recently, I thought Almae's son was named Esmund, but when Almae left him as a toddler at the Silverblood estate, she had changed his name.

A tall man wearing a black suit and a woman in a dark purple pantsuit entered the room. Keeran and Luana. The warlock had dark hair and dark eyes, and even though I could see plenty of Almae in him, I could also see Soren, and that turned my stomach. The alpha werewolf was a pretty woman with long light brown hair and hazel eyes. From what I had been told, she had become the alpha of the Starlight wolves, who shifted without tearing their clothes and glowed a bright purple.

Keeran and Luana smiled upon seeing their friends. Aurora ran toward Keeran, who caught her in his arms and gave her a tight squeeze. Drake walked to them, and the six of them exchanged hugs, friendly shoulder taps, and loving greetings.

"Keeran, Luana." Drake turned toward me. "This is Prince Killian DuMoir."

The warlock and the werewolf lost their smiles.

"I heard about what happened," Keeran said, his eyes grave. "I'm sorry for the suffering my mother and father caused you."

A wave of rage surged into me and I clenched my fists. It was all I could do to keep myself from tearing out his throat.

"We can assure you, the warlocks who took your mate are not working for Keeran," Luana said.

"You said you saw Tack, right?" Keeran asked, and I nodded. "From the information I could gather, we're dealing with Tack, Eldon, Damien, and Bates. They were the high-ranked warlocks under Soren."

My brows slammed down. I remembered those warlocks. Along with Virion, they were the ones who made Soren's inner circle.

"Isn't Virion with them?" I asked.

Keeran shook his head. "Virion is dead."

That made me curious, but I wasn't about to ask more when there were more pressing matters.

"We're assuming they took Lavinia because she can manipulate the boxes," Almae added.

"Manipulate the boxes?" The question was out of my mouth before I made sense of it.

Almae looked at me. "Before Delia fled with the boxes, I made sure only I could use them again. If she can open the boxes and absorb their magic, that means she has the same magic as mine running through her veins. She can do more than open and use the boxes. She probably can change them, transform them, and—"

"Destroy them," I whispered.

"It would be a complicated process, but yes." Almae nodded. "I think she would be able to do that."

"Do you think these warlocks know Lavinia can do all that?" Thea asked, her voice dripping with worry.

"I don't know," Almae said. "Either way, we know these warlocks mean to find all the boxes and activate the spell. We cannot let them do that."

"We have two of the boxes," Drake said. "They're not getting them."

"And we'll rescue Lavinia," Thea added, offering me a reassuring smile. "Somehow."

"Which reminds me ..." Almae took Keeran's hand in hers and pulled him back to the couch. They sat down. "Lend me a bit of your magic."

Keeran nodded. His grip tightened around Almae's hands. The witch closed her eyes and focused. Keeran watched his mother as she repeated one the spells she had been using for two days now, trying to locate Lavinia.

In silence, we all stood around the two of them.

After a few minutes, Almae swayed to the side, her head lolling.

"Mother!" Keeran cried, tugging on her hands. "Open your eyes."

"Killian, catch her," Aurora said suddenly.

For half a second, I was stunned by such command, but then I acted as Almae began to slip from the couch. With my vampire speed, I put out my arm and cradled her head and shoulders before they hit the floor. I pushed her back to the couch and Keeran held on to her arms this time.

"Thanks," he muttered.

Thea sat down on Almae's other side. "I think you need more rest. Come on. Let's eat something, then lay down."

Almae turned deadly eyes to Thea. "I don't want to rest. I want to find my niece!" She clamped her mouth, swallowing a half-sob. "I lost my sister, I will not lose my niece too." Her eyes welled with tears. "I need to find her."

Thea ran her hand over Almae's shoulder. "I know, my friend, but we already talked about this. If you kill yourself from exhaustion, you won't be able to help her at all."

Almae glanced at all of us. There was sympathy in everyone's gazes but mine. I didn't know how I felt about her and her actions. This wasn't the time for me to analyze it. I would do that after Lavinia was back, safe beside me.

Gently, Luana, Thea, and Aurora guided Almae out of the room.

Keeran let out a long sigh. "This is all so complicated."

I almost snorted. He could say that again. Twenty years ago, I had been plucked from my life, taken by warlocks who used me in a creepy spell and locked me in a magical box. A witch helped them, and this witch was the aunt of the witch who freed me, the one who turned out to be my mate.

Too complicated, too intertwined, too hard.

Drake nodded. "It is, but we'll deal with everything, one thing at a time, and we'll fix it all. First on my list is to make sure the boxes we have are secured. We'll gather later tonight with Thea and Elisa and make sure we have the strongest wards and spells around the boxes. No one will be able to get to them. Then, we find Lavinia." He paused. "Somehow."

Keeran's eyes widened. "When my father took Luana, he took her from Dark Witch Manor to the Château of the Cursed."

"And?" I asked, suddenly irritated.

"Soren told Luana he had plenty of hideouts throughout the entire world," Keeran said. "I've learned the location of a few, but there are more, I know that."

"You think they took Lavinia to one of these places?" Drake asked. I held my breath.

Keeran nodded. "All we need to do is search the locations."

"You just said you don't know all of the locations," I said through gritted teeth.

"True, but we can interrogate my warlocks again, see if we can connect the dots of what each one might remember," Keeran said. "We can ask my mother too. Soren trusted her. She might remember something. And, on top of all that, I can search Soren's old ledgers for information."

This was actually a good idea. If this worked, we could find Lavinia. But ... "What if they figured we would do this and chose some other place?"

Keeran shrugged. "There's only one way to find out."

True, and that was better than sitting here and waiting for a clue to land in my lap. I gave him a sharp nod. "All right, I'll help you if I can."

AFTER THE TALK WITH KEERAN, I was too worked up to join them for dinner. Instead, I went to the forest to hunt. Even though the castle was in lockdown, Drake had allowed me free rein to come and go, and thankfully, they kept a wildlife preserve nearby, so we could feed.

Once upon a time, DuMoir Castle was known for housing powerful lords who threw extravagant balls twice a year. People from all around the world applied for a chance to be one of the one hundred people invited to each ball. They were chosen carefully, mostly people who didn't have family or close friends, because once they entered the castle, they never left. We tricked the people, making them drink a spelled champagne. Some, we killed and drank from right at the ball, but most, we took them to our dungeons and treated them as our blood slaves. We tried to make them last for six months, until we had another ball and brought in another hundred clueless guests.

The last one of those balls had been almost seven years ago, when Thea had come to the castle and a war started.

Since then, everything changed. Now, we had plenty of blood bags from donation centers in the castle's freezers, and the wildlife was carefully maintained so we could drink from animals.

It wasn't the same thing—it would never be—but since getting out of the cursed box, I had been drinking from animals anyway. I was already used to it.

I walked out of the castle and ran into the forest. I stopped inside and listened—a broken twig, a broken leaf ... there! A deer. I followed my senses and found the deer. I didn't even give it a chance to see me, to react to my presence. In a second, I took it down and had my fangs around its thick neck.

I drank the warm blood, filling my veins with its sweet taste, gaining energy I so desperately needed. When I was done, I let the body drop to the ground with a heavy thud.

The blood made me feel alive again, hopeful, almost in a state of ecstasy. The only thing better would be drinking from Lavinia.

Lavinia ...

My shoulders sank and a pang cut through my chest.

This was too damn hard and I didn't know how to make it easier. How to find her faster. I felt useless.

I heard his slow breathing before he tried to pounce on me.

I spun out of the way as Shane, in his wolf form, jumped at me. He landed beside the dead deer, a snarl on his ferocious face. I bared my fangs at him. And he came at me again. I ran as fast as I could, and he gave pursuit. He was faster than I was.

We exited the forest, the castle looming in front of us, and I slowed down. Shane jumped from the line of trees, swiped his big claw at my head again, then shifted back into his human form.

"One of these days, I'll get you," he said as he turned to a tree at the edge of the forest. Naked, he crouched down and picked up the black jeans and blue shirt he had left there. He got dressed and turned to me again. He had cut his hair and shaved recently; he looked a lot younger now. "Feeling better?"

I lifted a shoulder. "A little."

Shane snorted. "Liar."

I frowned. I understood why Twyla stayed here—she was connected to the boxes like I was. But I didn't understand Shane. What was holding him here? No one would push him away, but still, it was odd to have a wolf shifter in a coven of vampires.

We walked toward the castle. A few clouds trailed through the night sky, and every few minutes the moon peeked out, shining down on the dark turrets. It was the second week of November and we were expecting a snowstorm soon. That would probably make looking for Lavinia even harder.

I let out a long sigh and glanced up to the castle.

Twyla stood in front of the second floor's library window. She looked down at Shane and me, and then retreated.

I frowned. "Have you talked to her today?"

Shane shook his head. "I've tried, but she doesn't open her bedroom door for me. I tried catching her when she went to the library this morning, but she ignored me."

"She doesn't seem to be happy about her situation." Honestly, I couldn't blame her.

"Is there anyone happy here? Now, I mean?" Shane gestured to the castle. "Lavinia is missing, some mad warlocks want to enact a dangerous spell, and a war is brewing."

He was right. Even the happiest of supernaturals living in DuMoir Castle had a dark storm brewing over their heads right now.

"I just want Lavinia back," I whispered, the words out before I could give them thought.

"I hear you. I'm worried about her too. If there was only a way of finding out more, of following a trail ... but we already searched everywhere around the castle."

Something about what he said sparked in my mind. Maybe we could find out more and follow a trail. I halted and turned to him, my eyes wide. "I have an idea."

4

KILLIAN

I GLANCED AROUND THE VAULT. I'D THOUGHT THIS PLACE would be secure, but the open stone room had high ceilings and archways leading to tunnels snaking underneath the castle. Anyone could get into it.

The two black boxes were on a wooden shelf between two archways, shoved there among several other items that I had never seen before. It seemed DuMoir Castle had more treasures than I ever imagined.

I picked up the boxes, surprised by their weight. They weighed less than a feather, and their material was almost as smooth as velvet. I had touched them before, briefly, but I still expected them to be heavier, rougher. I held tight to the boxes and walked out of the vault, taking the main tunnel back to the castle. There were no guards, no vampires around at this time of the night—on purpose.

I kept my senses open and headed toward the library, where protective cases would be waiting for the boxes.

I felt the sizzling in the air and jumped out of the way. Fat oily drops fell on the stone floors. Smoke rose from them as the stone melted, opening holes in the floor.

That could have been my skin.

I gritted my teeth and looked up, at where the liquid had come from.

A young vamp was pressed to the high ceiling, like a freaking spider. He hissed and ran to the nearest opening.

Drake, Thea, Cain, Shane, Keeran, Luana, Elisa, and Zadkiel emerged from the shadows and blocked his way.

Thea waved her hand and blue chains appeared around the vampire's wrists and ankles. He fell face-first on the floor.

I lowered my arms, the illusion of the boxes disappeared, and I stood over the young vampire. I grasped the collar of his shirt, baring my fangs at him. "You were after the boxes. Why? Who are you working for?"

His eyes rounded and his face paled. "I ... I ..."

I closed my hand around his throat, pulling him up until his feet were dangling in the air. "There's no half answers here, scum. You'll tell me what I want to know or—"

"Killian," Drake said, his voice low.

I gritted my teeth, my fangs aching to rip out the flesh of his throat and let him bleed out. I lowered the young vampire to his feet, but I didn't let go of his throat. Neither did I loosen my grip. "Who are you?"

The young vampire shook his head as best as he could while I squeezed his pipes.

"His name is Ballein and he's new," Cain said. "Well, new for a vampire. Holden and Elder found him in the woods two years ago. He had been attacked by a bear and was bleeding out. Because our numbers are still low, they brought him here, turned him, and trained him." Cain narrowed his eyes. "Though, he always complained about it all. He hated the training and tried to excuse himself from any responsibilities."

"So ... he doesn't like being a vampire," Drake said as matter of fact. He approached the young vampire and me. "Tell us, boy, is this true? You don't like being a vampire?" Drake nodded at me, and reluctantly, I eased up on my grip.

Ballein inhaled deeply and spat on Drake. Super-fast, Drake moved out of the way before the saliva could hit him.

I growled and pushed the scum against the wall. "You little—" I snapped my teeth right at his face. "Why did you do it? Who are working for?"

Though his face and body told us he was shitting his pants, Ballein stood his ground. "I-I'm not saying anything. Just kill me and get this over with."

I kneed his gut as hard as I could. Ballein's face went purple as he fought for air and pain spread over his body.

Thea appeared beside me. She pressed two fingers to the young vampire's chest. She muttered words under her breath. Then, she took two steps back and asked, "Who you're working for?"

Ballein's eyes glazed over. "I don't know."

I frowned. "Why did you try stealing the boxes?"

"I was sent a note saying that the boxes would be moved this evening," Ballein said, his tone almost robotic. "I was told that if I could steal the boxes and bring them deep into the forest, someone would be there to meet me and hand me a potion."

"What potion?" I asked.

"To make me human again."

Thea shook her head. "There's no such thing. Nothing can make a vampire human again."

"So someone used him," Drake said.

"Where's the note?" I asked, thinking we could see the handwriting, match it to someone. Or use it to track whoever was behind this.

"I was instructed to burn it," Ballein said.

Shit. I grazed my fangs over my lips. "Where were you supposed to meet this person?"

"At the edge of the forest, to the west, where the thick line of trees opens up to a cliff that overlooks the road beneath."

I stilled. "I know where that is." I glanced at Drake. He nodded. I let go of Ballein and ran out of the castle. I heard as others followed me.

I raced through the forest, faster than I had ever run before. My eyes adjusted to the darkness, and I barely saw the trees as I zipped past them. I halted behind the thick tree line Ballein mentioned and spied out. A few seconds later, Shane, Cain, and Luana appeared beside me—both shifters in their wolf forms.

We spied through the trees.

A figure stood right at the cliff's edge, with dark clothes and a dark cloak billowing in the breeze.

A warlock.

I ran to him.

The warlock threw his hand to the side. Dark lines appeared in front of him, forming a circle in the air. He jumped in it—a portal.

"No!" I shouted.

The portal closed, and the warlock got away.

5

LAVINIA

THE NEXT MORNING, A SHORT WARLOCK WITH SHAVED HEAD and tattoos on his neck escorted me from my bedroom to the summoning room.

There, Eldon, Tack, Damien, and Bates waited for me.

My hands shook, afraid of what they would have me do today, or what pain they might inflict on me, but I hid my hands behind my back and lifted my chin. Once more I held on to rage and pushed back my fear.

"We have a fun task today," Eldon declared.

I didn't say anything. There was nothing I considered fun here.

Tack picked up the prototype from the table. "We've located another box."

My stomach dropped.

No ...

Eldon looked me up and down. What was so special about jeans, a sweater, and boots? Then he glanced over my shoulder. The bald warlock still stood there. "Bring her a thick jacket, snow cap, and gloves, Chess."

Chess walked out of the door.

I frowned. "Wait ..." It dawned on me. "You're taking me with you."

It wasn't a question.

Damien answered it anyway. "Of course. Now that you're here, this part will be easier."

I narrowed my eyes. "What do you mean?"

"You'll see." Eldon reached behind me and grabbed the coat from the warlock. I hadn't even seen Chess come back. "Put this on. You'll need it."

He shoved the jacket into my hands before turning around and picking up a thick, wool-lined cloak from a pile on a chair in the corner. Tack, Damien, and Bates picked theirs up and donned them.

Another three warlocks came into the room, all wearing that same cloak. Chess handed me a wool beanie and thick waterproof gloves.

Holy shit, were we going to Everest? If that was the case, then the most impressive thing about all of this was that Delia had gone there to hide the box.

Eldon stepped to the center of the room and moved his hands in a fast, swirling sequence. Black lines appeared in the air in front of him and stretched wide, forming a vertical circle lined by odd runes.

A portal.

"Let's go." He stepped through it.

Tack gestured toward me. "You're next, witch."

I hesitated. I didn't want to go, but I knew that if I resisted, it would only cause me pain. I inhaled deeply, put on the jacket, the beanie, the gloves, and stepped into the portal.

The cold hit me at once, burning my face and chilling my bones. I squinted, the sudden brightness blinding me. I peeked through my lashes, and my vision adjusted to the light.

I fully opened my eyes and gasped.

Snow ... there was snow, and mountains, and a bright blue sky everywhere.

In the valley below the mountain was a smoking lake with crystal-blue water.

A hot spring.

"Where are we?" I asked in awe.

"Chile," Damien said. Along with Eldon, he stepped onto a narrow stone path that led down the mountain.

"Watch your step," Bates said as he took the path too. "The stones are slippery."

I frowned. If I didn't know better, I would say he cared if I got hurt. I rolled my eyes and forced my feet to move. The idea of the warlock who had kidnapped me caring was so ridiculous, I pushed it from my mind.

Eldon, Damien, Tack, and Bates took the lead, while the other four warlocks took the rear—and I was between them.

I sighed and focused on my steps, careful on the slippery rocks and the bits of ice and snow dusting them. Instead of dreading about what we were about to do, I took in the beautiful view, the crisp air, the chill breeze that blew every few seconds, and the shy sun that shone bright but couldn't warm us.

We reached the lake's bed and the warlocks spread out, forming a line beside me. Without a word, they moved their hands in the same pattern, their eyebrows curled down, their faces twisted in concentration.

Then, like Moses and the Red Sea, the warlocks pushed their hands out and the lake parted right in the middle, a dry corridor leading to the center of the lake.

Straining, Eldon looked at me. "In the center, the box is buried there. Get it."

I stared at him. "Me?"

"Yes, you," he said through gritted teeth. "It'll be easier that way."

I frowned. "But—"

"No buts!" he shouted. I stilled. "Do it now, before I force you there and drown you in the lake. It might look great, but this spring has a temperature of 110 degrees. With the shock of being out in the cold, I bet you'll at least feel horrible pain when the water surrounds you. Now, just do it."

I swallowed hard.

I knew I couldn't argue with the warlocks. If I did what they asked, it would be faster and easier, painless. If I didn't, then I would suffer and would end up doing everything anyway.

So, I faced the corridor in front of me, the ground a mix of rocks and mud, and slowly made my way in. Bates and Damien moved in behind me, their hands spread out in front of them, as if that was the only thing keeping the wall of water up.

Shit. I hurried my steps, even when my boots sank deep in the mud and my jeans got wet and dirty. Even when my foot sank so fast, I fell on my knees and hands and splattered mud everywhere.

Groaning, I pushed to my feet and ripped the dirty gloves from my hands.

I trudged along several yards until I felt it. The sensation hit me hard and fast, like lightning cutting through my chest. It took my breath away.

A box. A box was calling me.

Damn it, they really could track them.

Following the box's call, I took three more steps and halted before a big rock half sunken into the mud.

"She's through," Damien said, his voice loud.

"Tell her to hurry up!" Tack shouted back from somewhere outside the spring.

I glanced at Damien. "What do you mean I'm through?"

"The wards," he told me. "It would've taken us hours to break through them."

And I was able to simply walk through them and not feel a thing. Not because it had been Delia's magic around the box, but because the box was connected to me.

It wanted me to find it.

I reached for the rock, sinking half of my hands in the mud, and pulled. The rock barely budged. Inhaling deeply, I called my magic and let the power fill me with its potency. I rejoiced in the wonderful sensation for a brief moment, then used my magic to lend me strength. I easily lifted the rock and pushed it aside.

I put the gloves back on and ... I didn't know how I knew, but I simply pushed my arm through the mud where the rock had been, until it reached my shoulder. My fingers closed around something hard and rectangular. I pulled it out of the dirt and stood. Mud covered it, but I held in my gloved hands another box.

I stared at it, in awe that I had found another one, and in fear. Now the warlocks had three damn boxes.

"She got it!" Bates yelled.

"Then come back and let's go," Eldon shouted.

"Let's go," Bates said to me.

I nodded and marched back through the corridor. Once the three of us were safely out of the spring's bed, the warlocks lowered their hands as one. The water walls rushed down and crashed together, forming huge waves. I stepped back so I wouldn't be splashed.

Eldon grabbed the box from me. He looked at it as if I had plucked a brick-sized diamond from the ground. "Another step closer."

THE WARLOCKS OPENED a portal and we popped back into their mansion. We discarded our dirty cloaks, jackets, gloves, and boots to the side, but before I could head to my bedroom for a warm shower and clean clothes, Tack grabbed my arm and pulled me to the center of the large white circle on the floor.

Eldon stepped in front of me and offered me the new box, now cleaned of all mud. It was like the other four boxes—a rectangular black stone with smooth sides. It didn't look like more than a polished piece of rock or a painted brick.

Again, I hesitated. I didn't want to touch it, didn't want to have anything to do with it. If I could, I would have stopped all of this from happening. But I couldn't, and if I refused, Eldon would use his magic to twist that damn potion that ran through my veins and make me suffer until I agreed.

To save me some pain, I held my breath and reached for the box.

My fingertips brushed it, and it changed. The ridges appeared, bright lines shone through them. The box shook and Eldon set it on the floor and stepped back, outside the circle. The box opened and smoke came out, filling the air around us.

I retreated as the smoke faded and a form appeared in the middle of the circle.

A low snarl echoed through the room.

Before the smoke was gone, I already knew what supernatural the box held.

The russet werewolf snapped its sharp teeth at me. It jumped. I rushed back and raised my hands, ready to throw something at the wolf, but it wasn't needed. The wolf hit the invisible wall of the circle and fell back. It tried two more times, becoming more hurt and dazed with each hit. After the fourth one, the wolf fell and didn't get up.

Its form changed to a naked woman with long dark hair, lying on the floor unconscious. I grabbed one of the clean cloaks from a chair and covered her body with it.

"What the hell are you doing?" Eldon asked, his voice harsh. He walked to my side and glared at me.

"You don't expect her to walk around naked, do you?" I barked back.

"Of course not." He kicked her hard in the stomach, pushing her back a few inches—enough for her to touch the open box behind her.

Smoke swirled around her. She was sucked back into the box. The smoke disappeared and the box closed with a definite click.

Mouth hanging open, I stared at the box, then at Eldon. "Why did you put her back?"

"Because we don't need her right now." He took a step closer and towered over me. He was trying to intimidate me and he was succeeding. "You don't ask questions around here."

He picked up the box and placed it on one of the points of the circle. Three done, two more at DuMoir Castle. That was one-third needed for the spell. At this rate, Eldon and his warlocks would be able to finish it in a couple of months.

An icy chill coated my skin.

I couldn't allow that to happen, but I didn't know how to stop them, not when they could control me.

Tack walked past me. "Go back to your bedroom. Bates, take her."

Bates stepped to my side and gestured for me to go with him. I didn't move right away, glued to my spot and a little scared of how things were moving too fast and spiraling out of control.

My chest hurt as I turned and followed Bates out of the room.

Halfway through the mansion, I felt it again. The pull, the call, the allure. The box was calling for me. And this damn box had a supernatural inside it. I could use it. I could absorb its magic, I could take it all into me, I could become—

I halted those thoughts and did my best to ignore those feelings.

The warlocks had one active box and the pull was strong ... what would happen once they had two, three, four? When they had all of them?

I wasn't sure I could resist them then.

6

LAVINIA

For the next two days, I was allowed to move through the villa, Chess or some other warlock trailing me, but I couldn't leave the mansion or wander too much.

As much as I hated to admit, it was boring to sit in my room and do nothing. Of course, I used that time to try to come up with a plan to escape, or destroy the boxes they had, or maybe destroy the prototype, but nothing I planned panned out. Every time I tried to find a way, a clue, something, anything that would let me escape this place, my plans were foiled. The warlocks saw it all and stopped me.

And, whenever possible, they inflicted pain through the potion in my veins.

They weren't stupid.

On the third day, Eldon called for me. Chess was the one who escorted me to the summoning room, then left me there with the other four warlocks—Eldon, Tack, Damien, and Bates. Though nobody talked to me much here, in these past couple of days, I learned that the four of them had been the most trusted warlocks within Soren's circle, along with Virion, who died a long time ago. When Keeran defeated Soren, the four warlocks escaped. They came to this villa, where they had increased their numbers by finding other lost warlocks around the world.

When they fled, they took the prototype box with them. And when I opened the first box, Killian's box, the prototype activated. That was how they sent the demons to retrieve the box and me in the forest when Killian and I were trying to hide his box. That was also how Tack and the others found us at the inn.

It seemed to be impossible to get rid of them.

I walked into the room but didn't step into the circle. Though it was a special circle for the spell with the boxes, they had trapped the werewolf inside a couple of days ago. If they wanted, they could trap me. I was tired of being a toy in their hands.

I crossed my arms and faced the warlocks.

With a wide, wicked grin, Eldon stepped aside and gestured to the floor behind him.

A box sat on a previously empty point.

I sucked in a sharp breath. I looked around—four boxes. They had four boxes.

"H-How?" I asked, confused. I thought that after the last time, they would want me to go on all of these trips.

"While we were in Chile, we sent a team to an island in Brazil," Eldon explained, pride echoing from his words.

I pressed my lips tight. This was going too fast. "Hm, I thought it was easier when I went with you."

"True, but this way, we're twice as fast. Besides, the wards are tricky, but we can break them."

Shit. This wasn't going well.

"So ..." Anger over fear, anger over fear. I exhaled, trying to loosen up a little. "I'm here so you can gloat you have another box, or what?"

"Actually, while we're planning for the next two boxes, I thought we could start on the next part of our plan." Eldon gestured for me to come closer.

I didn't.

Damien pressed his hand firmly between my shoulder blades and pushed me forward. I stumbled into the circle. "W-what are you doing?"

Eldon picked up the new box. "Lavinia, absorb the magic from this box."

I opened my mouth, sure I had heard him wrong. He didn't know what he was talking about. If I touched the box, if I used its magic ... I shook my head.

Damien grabbed my hand and pulled it toward the box. I jerked it from his grip and took a step back. "No, I—"

Eldon twisted his hand and pain assaulted me. It started deep in my core and spread through my body like wildfire. I fell on my knees as a scream rose to my throat, but I refused to let it out. I gritted my teeth and breathed through my nose, enduring the fire burning inside me.

Then, the pain was gone.

Eldon leaned over me. "Use the box's magic or we'll keep doing that until you do."

Tears sprang to my eyes, but I blinked them away. Anger over fear.

I pushed to my feet on wobbly knees and took a deep breath to calm myself. "I don't need to touch the box for that," I said, my voice faint.

Eldon nodded. "Then do it."

I looked at the box in his hands, my mind racing, trying

to find a solution for this, a way out, but there was none. There was nothing I could do at this moment.

Damien grasped my arm with a steel grip and hissed in my ear, "Do it now, witch, before I inflict pain."

"I'm focusing," I lied.

He let go of me but didn't step away, his body a couple of inches from mine. I wanted to recoil, disgusted with his proximity, but I held my ground. The less weakness I showed these men, the better.

"Hurry up," Tack snapped.

All right, I couldn't lie about this. "The new box isn't calling to me. There's probably no supernatural inside it. If there's no one inside it, there's no power for me to absorb."

"All right." Eldon put the new box back in its place and picked up the werewolf box. "Now do it."

Damn it.

I sucked in a long breath and closed my eyes. I had felt the box calling for me since we first found it. It was easy to follow the call, open myself to it, and dip into its power. The box's magic didn't resist me at all. It came to me, fast, hard, and unbidden. It filled my veins, my muscles, my pores. It entwined around my own magic, making it stronger.

Darker.

This sensation, this feeling ... it was pure power, pure strength, and so delicious.

And I wanted it all.

KILLIAN

I PACED IN FRONT OF DRAKE'S DESK. THAT HAD BECOME A habit I couldn't shake. It had been three days since Lavinia had been taken, and we were no closer to finding her.

Deep down, I knew the warlocks wouldn't hurt her. What Drake had told me about them needing her was true. Still, that didn't make me any less worried.

And I loathed being here, waiting.

"I can't take this anymore," I said through gritted teeth.

"I know." Drake stood by the narrow end table to the side of his office, where a silver tray with several bottles and glasses rested. He picked up a bottle of whiskey and poured a good dose in two glasses. He brought one glass to me and held on to the other. "That's why I'm sending you to a meeting."

I stared at him. "A meeting? Now? If it's not with the damn warlocks who took Lavinia, I don't want to." I grabbed the glass from him and downed the contents in one gulp.

"First, I confirmed we would be at this meeting months ago," Drake said. "Second, the Dark Devils will be there."

I froze. The Dark Devils. Twenty years ago, Soren and Almae created the boxes for the Dark Devils. Dommik, their leader, wanted enough power to defeat DuMoir Castle. He wanted us gone so he could rule the supernatural world.

What a prick.

If the warlocks had taken Lavinia so she could help them finish the spell, then it meant the Dark Devils were in it, too, right? They would be on standby, waiting to hear when the warlocks had all the boxes and could complete the spell.

I dropped the glass on Drake's desk and clenched my fists. "You think Dommik will go?"

Drake nodded. "We have this meeting every five years, to make sure all vampire clans in North America are 'behaving,' and Dommik has not missed a single one in over a century."

Those meetings. I remembered them. Lord Reynard used to go to most of them. If he couldn't go, he sent Drake or Alex. Sometimes, the three of them would go together, a show of force. Well, it worked.

I frowned. "Are you coming with me?"

Drake nodded. "As much as I would like to send just you, Cain, and Patrick to represent us, I think that if the Dark Devils are working with the warlocks again, we have to show them we're stronger than ever."

I bristled. He wanted to take Patrick too? I didn't like it, but I had been away for too long. Perhaps Patrick had changed, or he at least had become a good cog in Drake's well-oiled machine. I couldn't argue about that now.

"When is this meeting?" I asked.

"Tonight. We leave in two hours."

To my surprise, the shindig was located in a conference room at a fancy hotel in New York City. I had no idea who'd organized it, but there were valets waiting to take our cars, a security team of several kinds of supernaturals who checked us all for weapons and potions before entering, and the room was decorated in elegant black and silver colors. A string quartet played soft classical music in a corner, and servers walked around with silver trays filled with champagne flutes and hors d'oeuvres.

"Are all vampire meetings like this?" I muttered to Drake as we walked in. I was careful with my tone, knowing everyone here had excellent hearing.

"Well, vampires like to show off, so ..." Drake shrugged. "Besides, this was never a true meeting. It was more like a get together, to make sure we all got along. If an issue shows up, we stop the music, turn the chairs, and discuss."

My brow furrowed. "I'm sure we'll have things to discuss this time."

Drake shot me a warning look. On the way here, he had told me to be careful. He didn't want me to question the Dark Devils about the boxes out in the open, because that would make others interested, and the last thing we needed was the vampire covens turning on each other.

A female vampire in an elegant black dress showed Drake, Cain, Patrick, and me to the center table. Another vampire showed up with an expensive bottle of champagne and a bottle of "red wine"—that wasn't wine.

I recognized most faces in the room, but there were a couple of new ones, most of the new vampires who had come with their leaders.

Loud footsteps and laughter reached my ears. Drake, Cain, Patrick, and I looked at the big double doors as

Dommik and three of his vampires walked in. He looked like I remembered, but with a different hairstyle. Instead of a buzz cut, he now had his silver hair combed back and curling behind his neck. His dark eyes were sharp, and his mouth too wide for his face. But he was tall, strong, and dangerous.

And he knew it.

He sauntered to us. "Lord Drake, what an honor to be in your presence." He made a show of bowing his head. The three vampires with him did the same.

Drake stood up. "Stop mocking me, Dommik."

"Mocking you, my lord?" Dommik pressed a hand to his chest. "Never!"

A growl started low in my chest. Dommik looked at me. "By sweet blood, Killian! You're here! Last I heard, you were dead ... about twenty years ago."

I shot to my feet, taking a step closer to him. "That was in part your doing."

Dommik let his mouth fall open, as if he was surprised. "My-oh-my, that can't be true."

I advanced another step, but Drake put out a hand. I stopped.

"Dommik," Drake said, his voice low. "We know about your deal with Soren twenty years ago. We know he created a dangerous spell that would make you the most powerful vampire around."

Dommik tsked. "Not the most powerful vampire. The most powerful supernatural." He winked. "There's a big difference. However, you can't prove any of that, can you?"

"I'm back, you bastard," I said through gritted teeth. " Soren's dead, but Acalla and I remember everything."

Soren wasn't really dead, but I didn't want to explain that to him.

Dommik's fake smile disappeared. "It's a shame that Soren lost the spell and it couldn't be finished. Otherwise, we would be having a different conversation right now." He narrowed his eyes at me. "I gotta say, I'm curious. How did you come back? I heard, hm, you were lost."

"How I got out of the box doesn't matter," I told him. "But be sure of this: you won't be able to finish the spell this time, and this time we'll make sure it's gone forever."

Surprise flashed in his dark eyes. It was only for half a second, but I had seen it before he schooled his features. "Of course, little vamp. Of course." He looked back at Drake and bowed his head again. "Now, if you'll excuse me, I plan to enjoy the meeting."

With a final glance in my direction, Dommik and his vampires walked to their table, where they opened the blood bottle and nearly drained it in three seconds flat.

Drake and I sat back down. The four of us exchanged grave glances.

"You had to open your mouth about the boxes?" Patrick hissed.

"As if he didn't know," I argued.

"It didn't seem like he did!" Patrick said.

"Even if he didn't know, there isn't much he can do about it," Cain said. "Unless he knows where to find the warlocks."

Drake nodded. "Right. We should put some shadows on Dommik and his vampires for a few days. See if any of them lead us to the warlocks."

"Can't I pull his teeth out instead?" I asked, my temper rising.

"As satisfying as that might be, I'm trying to show a more controlled side of DuMoir Castle," Drake said. "Controlled, but still very much in power. So, no, no torturing him. At least not for now."

I picked up my glass of champagne and downed it. If I was going to endure an entire night with Dommik only a few yards from me, I would need all the champagne I could get.

8

———

LAVINIA

I STRODE INTO THE SUMMONING ROOM, THE SKIRT OF MY beautiful dark red dress swooshing around my legs and revealing a hint of skin through the thigh-high slit in the fabric. My silver heels clicked against the stone floors, and giant diamond earrings glittered at my ears.

"Dressed to impress," Tack said, appraising me. "That should do it."

Eldon frowned at me. "Are you ready?"

I nodded.

"Let's open the portal," Eldon ordered.

He, Tack, Damien, and Bates opened a portal for me.

"You know what to do." Eldon beckoned toward the portal.

I offered him a half-smile before I stepped through and onto the neatly manicured lawn of a gorgeous stone manor in the heart of London. A higher demon lived in this house and had found a box when traveling. The demon was a collector like Taedon and Boristen. He could absorb a little of the box's power, even though he had no idea what it was and how he could do it. The box had become his most valuable item and was now displayed on a pedestal in the center of his collection room.

"I'll be here," Tack said from my side.

He had come with me, a bag slung from his shoulder—a bag with the four boxes we had. I didn't even need to open my senses to feel them anymore. My magic was now so attuned to them, I could tap into their power as if I was tapping into mine. They just had to be close by, and I could use them.

Only one of the boxes had a werewolf in them, but since tapping into its power, I now could feel the others too. All of them had been made with an incredible amount of power—power that had been absorbed by them, had grown with time, and which I stole back.

They fed into my power, strengthened my connection to them. I was glad they were all so close to me.

My gaze lingered on the bag, my fingers itching to touch them.

"Go," Tack urged.

I blinked. Yes. My mission. I had to go.

I rolled my shoulders and walked to the manor. I went up the four stone steps and the big glass door opened wide for me. Music rolled through the foyer and the living room, and the guests all halted their chatting and laughter to glance at me.

With a smile, I walked in. I looked around. Even with all this power, I couldn't sense the supernaturals, but I had seen a wolf shifter to the right, and another witch at the second-floor landing, which opened to the foyer's high ceiling. The rest of the guests seemed to be humans.

Then I sensed him. The higher demon. The seemingly

human man walked into the foyer from the dining room to the left. He looked like a billionaire with his three-piece suit and fancy updo, but I knew better. He was evil, the grandson of the previous Supreme Demon, and a thorn in my side.

Tegard stopped when he saw me. "Who are you? What are you doing here?"

My smile turned vicious. "Tell them to go, or they will get hurt."

"What?" he asked.

I answered his question by calling my magic. Blue flames enveloped my hands and arms. "I won't say it again."

Screams rang out through the manor. The humans ran toward the exits, and even the wolf and the witch left without helping the higher demon.

When the place seemed cleared, the demon approached me. "What do you want?"

"The box."

"What box?"

I could feel it calling for me, waiting, wanting ... I threw the flames at him and he jumped aside to deflect them. I followed the call to a door under an archway. I opened it and was greeted by a wide stone stair. I went down and found myself in the vast collections room—there were statues, bronze busts, old weapons, golden vases, huge paintings ... and right in the center, the box.

I walked toward it.

Tegard stepped in front of me. "Hear me, little witch. This is not a box. This is a stone, and it's mine." He opened up his legs hip-width. Ready for battle. "You're not taking it."

Oh, he was so stupid.

In three seconds, I welcomed my magic, the magic from

the box Tack held outside the manor, and the box standing a few feet from me.

With their combined magic, not even a damn higher demon was a match for me.

My lips curled up, and I made a sweeping move with my arm. Blue magic washed over the demon, sending him flying to the side. He hit some statue, the sound of clattering and breaking echoed through the room.

I pulled out a handkerchief from the cleavage of my dress and reached for the box.

The demon rammed into me, his body and strength enhanced because of his demon magic. I braced myself and skidded to the side, but with the magic within me, I created invisible anchors. After two feet, the demon couldn't push me anymore.

Eyes wide, he took two steps back. "*What* are you?"

"Wouldn't you like to know?" I threw both my hands at him and magic shot out from my palms. The blue flames enveloped him, much hotter than fire, and burned the demon's skin in seconds.

His scream was the only sound in the entire estate.

I wrapped the handkerchief around the box and cradled it in my arms. I turned to go, but halted in front of the dying demon. A smile took over my lips. That was how powerful I was now, and with the magic of this box and all the other boxes I would find, I would be even more.

I liked that.

I left the room, walked out of the house, and dropped the box inside the bag Tack was holding. He watched me, a frown between his brows.

"No congratulations?" I teased.

He didn't say a word as he opened the portal and we stepped inside.

Eldon, Damien, and Bates waited for us in the summoning room. They glanced from me to Tack, then back to me.

"And?" Eldon asked.

"She got the box and killed the higher demon," Tack reported, sounding almost upset. "It was too easy."

A giant grin stretched over Eldon's face. "Well done." He reached for the bag and spied inside.

"What now?" I asked, impatient. I wanted to go out there again, find another box, take more power.

Holding the new box in his hands, Eldon fixed his dark gaze on me. "Now, witch, you're almost ready."

ELDON PLACED the boxes in the circle—five of them. Exactly one-third of the way. If we continued like this, we would soon have all fifteen ... *I* would have them all.

He and the other warlocks stepped out of the circle. "Take in their magic," he said.

He didn't have to tell me twice.

I opened myself up and reached for the new box ... oh, this time I didn't even have to try. The box's magic came to me, fast and eager, and filled me with pure power.

Pure darkness.

I wanted it. I wanted this delicious power, I wanted to consume it all, forever, and no one could stop me.

"Lavinia," someone said.

I turned and glared at the four figures to my right. Who were they? Nuisances who stood in my way. Supernaturals who were here to take my boxes from me. To steal their magic.

I would never allow that.

I lifted my hand to—

My gut twisted and fire flowed through my veins. I screamed and fell on my knees, as the pain spread. My vision darkened and I could barely breathe.

Someone stepped into the circle. "Remember, with that potion in your veins, I own you." The pain retreated a little and I inhaled a deep breath. My vision cleared. Eldon leaned over me. "You can't hurt us. Try it again, and I'll make sure you experience pain like never before."

Was it possible to be in more pain?

I shook my head. No, it was okay. All I had to do was listen to him. If I did, I could continue absorbing the boxes' magic. And I couldn't give up on the boxes now.

I pushed to my feet and faced the warlock.

"Do you understand who's in charge here?" Eldon asked, his voice low.

"You are." There wasn't one inch of doubt in my being. Eldon was the boss, along with Tack, Damien, and Bates.

And they let me have my beloved boxes and their power.

One corner of Eldon's lips curled up. "Now, you're ready."

KILLIAN

I WIPED MY MOUTH AS I CAME OUT OF THE FOREST—I HAD been so tense and angry, I had played with my food before killing it. I purposely chased it for almost half an hour. If I hadn't killed it, the poor deer would have died of exhaustion and a heart attack.

I glanced up at the darkening sky. It was getting chillier and chillier, and soon we would see the first snowfall. The forecast had promised a snowstorm, but it had just missed us, wreaking havoc about fifty miles north of here and upstate.

Last night, after we came back from the vampire covens' meeting, I couldn't sleep. So I went running with Shane to burn off my pent-up energy. I had fed then, and I fed now. My anger fueled my hunger.

I hated having all this time on my hands. I kept my mind busy, always trying to come up with a scenario or clue about where Lavinia could be and how I could find her. Keeran had interviewed most of his warlocks and sat down with Almae to list the hideouts Soren had had years ago. So far, the list was seven items long, and we had already checked all seven places. There was no sign of Lavinia, or anyone else, in any of those places. Almae was sure there were at least another four or five places she couldn't remember, or she didn't know about, so she spent her time switching from trying to find Lavinia through her foresight magic, and digging through her past to find such places.

Meanwhile, I waited like a damn fool.

If it depended on me, I would burn the whole world down in search of my mate, but what good would that do? That would take forever, and I would hurt innocent people in the process.

I heard her frantic heartbeat three seconds before she burst through one of the castle's side door and into an open stone patio. Almae looked flustered as she ran to me, with Thea and Luana chasing after her.

"What happened?" I asked, confused.

"I ..." She stopped in front of me and caught her breath. "I saw her. Lavinia."

I froze. "What? Where? When?"

She closed her eyes. "I think I can locate her, but Killian ... I couldn't see her before, and now I can. Very clearly. It seems like a trap."

I clenched my teeth. "I don't care. I'm going after her." I walked past them, toward the castle.

"If you are, then you better assemble a team," Thea said, falling into step with me. "If it's a trap, at least you'll be prepared."

"I'm sure it's a trap." Luana caught up with us. "This is too easy."

I halted and glared at her. "I. Don't. Care."

She raised both her hands. "Hey, I know. I would feel the same in your position. I'm just saying."

I resumed walking, faster. More agitated. I wanted to hop in a car and drive away now, but they were right. We needed to get Almae to a map and assemble a team. Still, I wanted us out of here in thirty minutes.

"We have no time to waste," I urged. "Let's go."

DRAKE STOPPED the SUV about a mile from where Almae had last seen Lavinia, about fifteen minutes ago. From here, we could see the road winding down and disappear around a curve and a valley.

First, Almae had seen Lavinia walking beside a road in Pennsylvania, just outside Scranton. We filled five three-rowed SUVs and drove that way. With our senses and immortality, we drove a lot faster than the speed limit, and it took us only four hours to get there. But by then, Lavinia had moved and when Almae focused again, she had seen Lavinia five miles north. We followed Almae's lead to this abandoned-looking road.

"All right." I reached for the door's handle. "I'll go alone. If anything goes wrong, I'll send you a signal."

Drake nodded. "I'll have vampires closing in around you, just in case."

I wanted to argue because if this was a trap, I didn't want to put Lavinia, or anyone else, at risk. But I knew he wouldn't have it any other way.

I exited the car and ran down the road. In a flash, I was at the gates of the farm Almae had seen Lavinia at. It was almost midnight, but there were a couple of lights on. From here, I could hear five sets of heartbeats inside the main house and one erratic heart in the barn.

I ran there but forced myself to slow down when I was fifty yards away. No other heartbeats, no other sounds. There wasn't anyone else here. If this was a trap, it was a badly planned one.

Slowly, I opened the barn's door. There weren't any animals here, just a broken tractor, several tools, and a pile of hay. Her shallow breathing echoed in my ears as I approached the hay and found her sleeping behind it.

My heart squeezed.

There she was ... my mate. She looked so small, curled on her side, and jerking as if she was having a bad dream. She stirred and her long hair fell away. A purple bruise covered her jaw, and scratches marred her neck.

A wave of rage coursed through me.

Those freaking warlocks ... I would hunt them down, pin them to a pole, and use them as practice targets. I would torture them like they never imagined possible and I would enjoy every second of it.

But first, I had to take Lavinia to safety and make sure she was okay.

I knelt beside her, my fingertips brushing her cheek. "Lavinia." My voice broke when I said her name. A lump rose to my throat. "My love?" Lavinia jerked awake and scooted away from me, her eyes wide and wild. I lifted my hands and showed her my palms. "It's okay, Lav. It's me."

She stared at me for a long time. Then her bottom lip trembled. "Killian?" Her eyes brimmed with tears.

I wound my arms around her and pulled her to me. A sob shook her body and she buried her face in my neck. I inhaled her scent, so relieved she was back with me. Damn, I had been scared this day would never come. "It's okay, my love. You're safe now."

As I took Lavinia to the SUV, carrying her frail frame in my arms, Drake had the vampires sweep the area—there was no one else around. It didn't seem like a trap.

I sat on the second row of the SUV with Lavinia, and she instantly snuggled against me and slept. Drake and the others wanted to ask her what happened, where she had been, how she had escaped, but she was hurt and tired. Every time someone suggested waking her up to talk, I bared my fangs and made it clear no one would bother her until she felt better.

We drove back to the castle. When I brought a sleeping Lavinia in, Almae started crying in relief. I took Lavinia to my chambers and had Thea and Almae take a look at her—without waking her up for questions—to make sure she was okay. Thea used her magic to heal most of Lavinia's wounds.

"The rest will disappear in a few days," she said. "But besides a little hurt, tired, dehydrated, malnourished, and weak, Lavinia seems fine. Tomorrow, when she's feeling better, I would like to take another look at her."

I agreed to it and shooed everyone from my chambers.

I sat beside Lavinia in bed and watched as her chest moved up and down, and listened to her heart and her breathing, suddenly entranced by their sound. It was like the most beautiful song I had ever heard.

In the middle of the night, Lavinia woke up with a start and looked around frantically. I turned on the side table lamp and approached her. "It's okay, Lavinia. You're safe now." I slowly reached for her, taking her hand in mine. "Whatever happened, it's okay now."

She sniffed. "I ... I'm glad I'm here with you again." Her voice was faint and rough, as if her throat was hurt. She scooted until she was sitting on my lap.

I wrapped my arms around her and took in a deep breath. I kissed the top of her head and whispered, "I promise you, my love. I'll never let anyone else hurt you again."

10

KILLIAN

I barely slept at night. I lay down beside Lavinia while she slept in my bed, but every time I closed my eyes, a gripping fear took hold of me. What if I was dreaming and when I woke up she wasn't here? What if she disappeared again? What if she was an illusion created by the warlocks to toy with me?

I held her hand most of the night, and she didn't feel like an illusion.

In the morning, I didn't wake her up. I figured she was still tired of the whole ordeal she went through and needed every second to rest. But I ordered a lower-ranked vampire to send us food. I wanted to have something ready for her when she woke up.

Mid-morning, I stood by the window and peeked out the closed curtains. It was a gray and cold day, but I felt like the sun shone upon me. Finally, Lavinia was back with me.

I heard her breathing and heartbeat changing and turned to the bed. Lavinia stirred, turned to her side, and opened her eyes. In a flash, I was seated beside her.

"Good morning," I said. All I wanted was to hold her, to kiss her, to press my face to her neck and never let go. But I had no idea what she had gone through these past few days. I didn't want to scare her. "How are you feeling?"

"Better." She sat up in bed and sniffed the air. "I smell something sweet."

My lips curled up. "Yes, I had breakfast brought for you. I hope it's still warm." I brought the tray to the bed and uncovered her plate. "A cinnamon roll, butter croissants, scrambled eggs, milk, and juice." And everything was still warm thanks to the heating mat between the tray and the plates.

She picked up the cinnamon roll and pulled off a piece. "Did I sleep long?"

I shook my head. "No. It's only ten in the morning." I shrugged. "And what if you had slept all day? You need to rest."

She took another bite from the roll, chewed, swallowed. She inhaled deeply. "The others are waiting for me, aren't they? They probably want a full report of where I've been and what happened."

I stiffened. "They can wait. Take your time." I reached over and placed my hand over her knee. "No one will force anything out of you."

Lavinia showed me a small smile. "Thanks for being so caring. But this is important." She sighed. "I'll finish eating, take a shower, get dressed, and then we can meet the others. I'm ready to talk."

I frowned. "Are you sure?"

She nodded. "I would rather rip off the Band-Aid and be done with this." She placed her hand over mine. "And then we can put this behind us and move on."

I liked that idea.

LAVINIA TOOK her time getting ready. Unlike the witches and female vampires in this castle, she put on what she was comfortable in—skinny jeans, a thin sweater, and her combat boots. Her outfit clashed with my slacks and button-up shirt, but I didn't care. She could wear rags, she would still be the most beautiful woman I had ever laid eyes upon.

It was almost noon when we finally emerged and made it to the sitting room outside the royal wing, where Drake had told us to meet him.

Drake, Thea, Almae, Keeran, and Luana were already there, waiting for us. At first, I found it strange that Aurora wasn't glued to Thea's or Drake's legs, but Elisa and Mila, Silverblood witches, usually watched over the girl when Thea was busy.

Almae held back for as long as she could while Lavinia walked in, shyly greeted everyone, and was introduced to the Warlock Lord and the Starlight Wolves alpha, but then the old witch embraced her niece tight, tears in her eyes.

"By the spirits." Almae took Lavinia's hand and pulled her to one of the couches in the middle of the room. "How are you, my dear?"

Lavinia pressed her lips together. "I'm okay now," she said, her voice low. Her eyes met Drake's. "I don't want to waste your time, so I'll tell you what happened and answer your questions."

Almae frowned. "If you need more time, we'll understand."

Lavinia shook her head. "Waiting longer won't change anything. The sooner I get it all off my chest, the sooner I can forget about it."

Thea and Luana took places on the couch across the center table, Keeran sat in an armchair, but Drake and I remained standing. My nerves were a buzz. I wasn't sure I was ready to hear what Lavinia had to say.

"Would you like something before you begin?" Thea asked. "Maybe some tea? Or wine?"

"Or whiskey?" Luana asked.

Lavinia almost smiled at that, but then her lips curled down. "No. Thanks. I just ... I was on my way to see Almae and Thea when someone grabbed from behind and everything went dark. When I woke up, I was with the warlocks—Eldon, Tack, Damien, and Bates."

"Soren's men," Keeran said. "So it is them."

"Yes." Lavinia nodded. "They are holed up in one of Soren's hideouts and—"

"Do you know which one?" Drake asked.

Lavinia shook her head. "I ... I don't. I'm not sure they said where it was located. All I can tell us is that it seemed we were deep in a forest."

Keeran looked at Almae. "A forest. Does that ring a bell?"

Almae sighed. "I'm afraid not."

"The warlocks said they had been growing their numbers since they left Soren," Lavinia continued. "They took the prototype box with them." Almae inhaled sharply. "It doesn't act like the other boxes, but somehow, it's connected to them. With the prototype, they knew I had activated Killian's box, and that's how they found us."

"They can use the prototype to track the boxes?" Drake asked, his voice hard.

Lavinia nodded. "They have five boxes."

"What?" Almae paled. She looked at me, at Drake.

"That's not all ..." Lavinia hesitated. "Some of the boxes

are empty, and they know they will find empty boxes. I heard them talking about finding supernaturals to fill those boxes."

"Holy shit," I muttered under my breath.

"At this rate, they will finish the spell," Thea said.

"We have two of those boxes," Drake reminded us. "They won't be getting those."

"But that's too close," Keeran said. "Even if we protect these two boxes, we need to take the others from them."

Drake dipped his chin. "Agreed."

"My dear." Almae patted Lavinia's hand. "When we found you, you were hurt. What ... what happened? What did they do to you?"

Lavinia's brow furrowed. My gut clenched. "The first thing I did was attack them so I could run, but they put a spell on me so I couldn't use my magic on them. They asked me to open the boxes for them, to check on them, and when I refused—" She pursed her lips. "Let's say they showed me how bad things could be."

I walked to the nearest window, opened it up, and breathed in the chill air. I needed to calm down.

"How did you escape?" Keeran asked.

"The blocking spell was temporary." Lavinia looked at her hands. "I felt it losing its power over me. Before they could cast the spell on me again, I absorbed the power from the boxes and attacked." She looked up at me. "Then I ran as fast and far as I could. I didn't even think about the boxes. I should have taken them with me, at least a couple, but at the time, I wasn't thinking. I just wanted to get away."

"That's understandable, my dear," Almae assured her.

"Did you kill the warlocks?" Luana asked.

Lavinia shook her head. "I don't think so. I'm strong when

I have the boxes' power, but they are powerful too. I think I stunned them."

Though I wanted to see those warlocks with their head on pikes, I was glad Lavinia hadn't been the one to kill them. She was never a killer, and I didn't want her to start being one now.

"We found you near Scranton," Drake said. "Do you know which direction you came from? For how long you were running?"

Lavinia shook her head. "I was so scared, so out of my mind, I barely remember running." She smoothed her hands on her legs. "I just remember feeling tired, lonely, hungry … that's when I slowed down and realized I was running alongside a road."

Drake glanced at me. I knew he had left a team behind to sweep the area—in a fifty miles radius. I hoped they had found something by now.

Lavinia stared at the coffee table in front of her, her eyes dazed. She had just gone through a traumatizing experience and we were bombarding her with questions. She had done a wonderful job answering what she could, but it was time to end this.

"I think we could all use a break," I said, my tone not up for discussion. "If Lavinia remembers more details, she'll let us know, right?"

She blinked and glanced at me. "Right."

I offered my hand to her. Slowly, she slipped her hand in mine. "I'll take Lavinia for lunch, then she'll rest for a bit." I turned to Drake. "If you want, we can meet again in a couple of hours. You can ask her more questions then."

Drake nodded. "I'll also want to meet with you and the other princes this evening."

"Of course," I said.

I bid everyone goodbye and guided Lavinia out of the room.

She didn't seem focused as we walked through the castle. I led her to the outside, to the garden beside the maze, when she halted and looked at me with huge eyes. "Lord Drake said you have the two other boxes here. It's not safe. Someone should take them, hide them, destroy them. The warlocks will come for them ... for me."

I grasped her shoulders and steadied her. "Lavinia, the boxes are safe here. This castle probably houses the most powerful supernaturals on this side of the world, and the boxes are in a special room and well-guarded, under heavy supervision and strong wards. The warlocks can try to take them, but they won't succeed." I cupped her beautiful face and ran my thumb over the faint mark on her cheek. I was going to murder all those damned warlocks slowly and painfully. "You are safe here with me."

She looked into my eyes, but she didn't look the same. There was a hint of sadness in her eyes, something that wasn't there before. The events of the last few days had broken her.

Somehow, she would heal.

I wanted to kiss her so bad, to make love to her again, to show her the opposite of what she had experienced, to show her how she was the owner of my heart, of my life, but I was afraid of scaring her, of pushing too far.

I stepped back from her. I crouched down beside an ever-green flowerbed and grabbed two coneflowers. I entwined the two flowers tightly until they formed a delicate and beautiful bracelet—just like her.

I slipped the bracelet around her wrist.

She offered me a small smile. "This is so ... pretty." Her eyes filled with tears. "Thank you." She rose on her tiptoes and pressed a soft kiss on my lips. I groaned, desperate for more, but I forced myself to stay still. "Thank you."

I was glad she was finally back with me. "Anything for you."

I slipped my hand in hers, our fingers entwined, and I took her on a slow walk through the maze.

11

LAVINIA

I waited until I was sure Killian was sleeping. I opened my eyes and looked at his face in the darkness, only the moonlight coming from a crack in the curtains illuminating the room. He was a handsome man, a powerful vampire prince ...

I waved my hand, and my magic spelled him.

And now this handsome vampire prince would sleep deeply for several hours.

I stood from his bed and dressed.

Killian had insisted I sleep in his chambers. He had brought in a large trunk with my things from the guest bedroom, and I had found a decent pajama set in it. I had to admit, I was a bit disappointed he had been so respectful of poor, broken Lavinia and hadn't tried anything. My body remembered his, and I knew sleeping with him would have been amazing ...

But I wasn't here for that.

I put my jeans, sweater, and boots back on, tied my hair

into a tight ponytail, grabbed an empty bag from my trunk, and left the bedroom without a backward glance.

It was child's play to walk through the hallways undetected and to put the vampires standing guard to sleep with a flick of my fingers. I didn't know exactly where the boxes were located, but their call was strong enough for me to follow ... and the closer I got, the stronger it became.

In no time, I found myself in a series of tunnels underneath the castle. The entrance had been hidden, but nothing a little magic couldn't fix.

The tunnels were dark and something barked in my mind about that ... about being in the dark, but nothing registered. I created a small blue flame and set it floating beside me to illuminate my way. The tunnels split every few yards, like a maze, but since I was following the boxes' call, I didn't feel lost once.

I finally arrived at a locked iron gate. I easily unlocked it with my magic and pushed it open. I stepped in ... and was pushed back several feet, the electrical shock of a strong ward making my heart race.

Ridiculous ...

I halted right in front of the doorway and focused. I felt the immense magic inside me—my own and from the other boxes. They had stayed behind with the warlocks, but I had absorbed as much magic from them as I could before leaving.

Being away from them was painful, but I would have the original two in my hands. I could feel them from here, though I couldn't use them because of the ward.

I was about to change that.

I sent my magic toward the ward. It felt like a heavy curtain draped over the doorway. My magic smoothed over the curtain, stretching as far and wide as it could go. It traveled to the corners of the curtain and tried finding any corners, any folds, or rips that would let me in. Patiently, I covered the ward with my own magic, suffocating it, muffling it. Then there! My magic folded under a tiny corner. I focused on that small opening and sent my magic like an avalanche. The ward fought back, but it had been breached. There was nothing it could do.

The ward faded away.

A smile crept over my lips as I stepped into a vast and dark room. I split the blue flame hovering into half a dozen and fanned them around the room.

Oh, this was the vault—a big room with treasures and magical items.

And Killian's and Twyla's boxes.

I grabbed the long scarf I had shoved into my pocket and unfolded it while I approached the boxes, their call like a sweet nectar. I didn't dare absorb from them just yet, but my skin itched with anticipation.

I stretched the scarf and—

"I knew it," a voice said from behind me.

I turned around. Twyla stood at the vault's entrance, her dark eyes murderous.

I feigned innocence. "What?"

"That it was a trap. That you showing up meant something bad." She took a few steps closer. Even though it was the middle of the night, she had normal clothes on—slacks, and a button-up blouse. She looked like a damn shadow fae queen with her long, black hair, and delicate features. "You're here to take the boxes, aren't you?" She extended her arms to the side and black flames covered them. "I won't let you."

My lips curled up. "You won't let me?" I almost laughed.

"Twyla, I know you have been following me since I left my room. And thank goodness you did; otherwise I would have to go after you myself."

She stared at me. "What?"

I rolled my eyes. "Stupid shadow fae."

I didn't give her a warning. I barely gave her a second to register what was happening. My magic surrounded her like a snake, fast and deadly, and covered her, muffling her scream and dousing her magic. I touched her box—it shook and opened—and I pushed Twyla into it.

I saw the desperate look in her eyes before she disappeared in a tornado of smoke.

The box closed.

One down, one to go.

***

I WRAPPED the boxes in the scarf and put them inside the bag I had gotten from Killian's closet. I slung it across my shoulders and left the vault. I had left small magical Xs on the walls and turns I took, so I would know my way back. The Xs disappeared once I walked past them.

In no time, I crossed the hidden doorway and stepped into a main hallway in the castle—and came face-to-face with Elisa and Zadkiel as they strolled through the corridor, hand-in-hand.

They stopped and stared at me.

"What ...?" Elisa's question died on her lips when she saw the bag hanging by my side. "No!" A blue bolt appeared in her hands. "You're not going anywhere, not with the boxes!"

She threw the bolt at me. I easily waved my hand and her bolt turned into smoke before it reached me.

"You're no match for me," I told her. Especially now that I wouldn't hesitate to use the two boxes I had with me.

Elisa snapped her fingers and a dozen blue sparks traveled away from us. "The entire castle will know there's trouble and will be here in a matter of seconds." She called two more bolts, and Zadkiel stripped off his shirt and let his black wings out. "We won't let you go."

I grinned at her. "We'll see about that."

KILLIAN

"KILLIAN!"

I turned in bed and instinctively reached for Lavinia. A cold pillow and sheets greeted me.

"Killian, wake up!"

I forced my eyes to open, my body to sit up, but I felt like I was swimming in syrup, and drowning. No command from my brain to my body was working.

Panic seized my chest.

A hand landed on my shoulder, and it was as if a curtain had been pulled back, and I was allowed to move again. Gasping, I opened my eyes and shot up from the bed.

Shane brought his hands up. "Hey, easy, man."

I looked around. It was still dark out and the only light in the bedroom was the one coming from the open door leading to the hallway. But screams and other sounds reached my ears.

"What's going on?" I glanced back at the empty bed. "Where's Lavinia?"

Shane's brow furrowed. "Man ... You better come and see."

I didn't like the sound of that. Thankfully, I had gone to bed fully clothed—I didn't want to scare Lavinia by stripping off and lying beside her. At least not yet. I wanted her to come to me first, to show me she was okay.

But I had no idea where she was now and the apprehension gripping my heart grew tighter as Shane and I exited my room. The screams, the sounds of fighting were louder here.

Shane and I ran down the stairs, but a sea of blue flames covered the entire first floor.

"Shit, this wasn't here a minute ago," Shane said from the top of the staircase.

"What's going on?" I asked.

Shane didn't answer. Instead, he turned to the large window by the staircase. From here we could see the castle's front garden.

Lavinia was halfway across the entrance road, fighting at least two dozen vampires and witches back.

My stomach sank.

No.

Dark blue shadows and flames surrounding Lavinia. Drake, Thea, Keeran, Luana and others tried to subdue her, but she was too strong.

Pressure squeezed my lungs; my legs trembled. The breath was taken from me as sudden pain assaulted me. Lavinia created a blue wave that washed over her opponents.

She had absorbed power from my box ... and used it.

Her magic forced Drake and the others back, most of them stumbling on their own feet or falling to their knees.

Lavinia was too strong backed by the power of the boxes. They couldn't win.

She sent a second wave at them, then she turned and ran down the road. It took her opponents a few precious seconds to recover and start after her.

But by then, I knew she was gone. Pain stabbed the middle of my chest. A warlock must have opened a portal for her.

And she had taken my box with her.

I pressed a hand to my chest, still trying to make sense of it.

Lavinia, my mate, my love, the woman who had been made for me, had been brainwashed by the warlocks. That was the only explanation. Otherwise, she wouldn't do this. I knew that just as I knew my name.

"That's not her," I muttered.

Beside me, Shane nodded. "I agree, but man, there's more."

I looked at him. "What now?"

"Twyla is missing."

Holy shit.

Lavinia had taken Twyla.

13

LAVINIA

As soon as I crossed through the portal, Eldon took the bag from me. An urge to fight him rose in me but I pushed it down. Despite my power, he still had an advantage over me, one I couldn't control. I had to obey my master.

We entered the mansion and went to the summoning room. Eldon placed the other boxes in the circle.

He stepped back and admired the seven boxes we had gathered. "Now we have the fae and the vampire boxes complete."

"Hm, not complete," I said.

He turned dark eyes to me. "What do you mean?"

"I couldn't get Killian in the box," I said. "I was found out as I was making my way to him."

A vein in his forehead jumped. "You're saying there's no one inside the vampire's box?"

I looked at the shiny floor.

"Never mind that," Tack said. "We can find another vampire."

We could do that?

"Right," Eldon muttered. He approached the long, narrow table along the wall with Tack, and both of them messed with some things there, while speaking lowly.

I tuned them out and opened myself to the pull of the seven boxes. It was intoxicating. I knelt in the center of the circle, my butt on my heels, and closed my eyes, taking it all in.

So much power, so much darkness. If I let myself go, I could swim in a dark sea now and forever, sinking deep, deep, deep, and never come back for air again. I wanted it; I needed it. It fed me; it kept me going. It was my water, my bread, my energy.

I opened my eyes and found Bates standing in front of me, his eyes narrowed. What was it with him? He was always looking at me as if he knew better. Wasn't I doing what they wanted?

Chess entered the room. "We brought her in, my lord."

I frowned.

Eldon turned to Chess with wide, amused eyes. "Where is she?"

"In the basement," Chess said. "She wouldn't stop fighting; we had to sedate her."

Eldon nodded. "That's fine. We'll go see her."

Eldon, Tack, Damien, and Bates followed Chess out of the room. I stood to follow and hesitated. I wanted to go, but it was so hard to step away from my beloved boxes. If I could choose, I wouldn't take my eyes off them for half a second.

But my curiosity won.

Besides, I knew no one would take the boxes from this room. If they did, I would hunt them to the ends of the earth and cook them alive until they gave me the boxes back. And then I would kill them.

I followed the five warlocks to the basement. The basement looked like a normal room, but once we went down the narrow wooden stairs, I saw the wall of bars at the end of the large room—the front side of half a dozen cells.

One of them was occupied by a slumped figure in a thin blanket on the hard concrete floor.

I approached the cell. The warlocks had kidnapped a young woman with fair skin, silver-blond curls, and a slim body.

"What is she?" I asked.

"An angel," Eldon said.

"Her name is Ariella," Chess said. "She was scouting a group of demons when we found her."

"You said she put up a fight?" Tack asked and Chess nodded. "Then keep her sedated until we put her in a box."

Chess dipped his chin once. "Yes, sir."

Damien leaned into the bars and looked at the sleeping angel. "A little too slim for my taste, but she looks pretty." His smile stretched over his fat lips. "Chess, don't sedate her too much. I want her to cause trouble. Then I can give her some trouble back."

I looked at the angel.

Soon she would be inside a box, and I would be able to use her box and feed from her power. Who cared about what happened to her now? I shrugged and walked out, not caring if Damien had fun with her or not.

14

———

LAVINIA

When Eldon called for me, I thought he had either located another box, or he'd brought in another supernatural and wanted to show her or him to me.

I was amused when Chess escorted me to the dining room, where Eldon, Tack, Damien, and Bates sat at the long wooden table. The dark red walls clashed with the dark wood paneling on the bottom half, and a painting of a red sea took over most of the wall above a heavy buffet set. The room was dramatic and elegant, and I rarely ate here.

Seated at one end of the table, Eldon gestured at the chair to his right. "Sit."

After glancing at the other warlocks, who were spread out along the table, I followed his order. I was expecting him to tell me about a report while he ate his dinner, so I was surprised when one of the lower-ranked warlocks—I didn't care to remember his name—brought me a plate, utensils, and a goblet of red wine.

I stared at Eldon. "What is this?"

"I rarely see you eat," he said. "If you're going to keep

taking in the boxes' magics and fighting, you need more energy."

I frowned. Was this some kind of trick? The food was poisoned? Why was he being so soft on me now?

Tack groaned. "Just eat, witch."

I reached for my utensils and dug into the buttery steak. It was delicious; I almost moaned. When I ate, I ate whatever I could find in the kitchen, or what I had the patience to cook for myself, which wasn't much. I had never eaten the same thing or at the same time as the four coven leaders.

The entire time, I felt the boxes calling for me. I wanted to shove this meal aside and go to them. If I were allowed, I would sleep in the summoning room, even if I had to sleep on the hard, cold floor, just so I could stay close to them.

I frowned and asked, "We'll complete the spell Soren started for the vampires? Why not use the power from the spell for yourselves?" That was what I would do.

Eldon finished chewing and swallowing before answering. "Soren never intended to give the power to the vampires. He planned to use the boxes for himself, and we plan on doing the same."

"So ... you aren't working with the vampires this time?"

Damien snorted. "You're observant for a witch."

What did that even mean?

"No, we aren't," Bates said, his voice somber.

"But we have been talking to a vampire," Damien said, shooting me a bored look. "We knew there could be trouble with the vampire box. When time comes, we'll put him in the box instead."

I dropped my fork. "Will that work?"

"We think so," Tack answered. "Maybe the box would be more responsive to Killian since it's attuned to him already, but I believe the box doesn't really care who is in there, as long as it's the same species, for the sake of the spell."

"Once we have all the boxes and supernaturals and activate the spell, I'll take in the power," Eldon said. "I'll be the most powerful supernatural in the world, and no one will dare mock us or make us hide again."

As long as he didn't take the boxes away from me, he could destroy the moon.

The rest of dinner, the warlocks talked about their plans to retrieve the next two boxes, and someone mentioned having found a succubus for one of the boxes and ...

"A dragon shifter," Damien said. That caught half of my attention—the other half was always attuned to the boxes in the summoning room.

"Are you sure?" Eldon asked, full of interest.

Damien nodded. "I can't be one hundred percent until I go there and see for myself, but yes, reports say we might have found a dragon shifter."

"I thought they were extinct," Bates said.

"Thankfully, it seems they aren't." Eldon took a sip of his wine. "Otherwise, we wouldn't be able to finish the spell."

They moved on to a report about goblins and mermaids, but by then I couldn't focus anymore. The call of the boxes was hard to resist. By the time dinner was done and the warlocks left the dining room, I was about to peel off my own skin. Once I was left alone, I ran to the summoning room and sat down as close as I could to the boxes without touching them. I closed my eyes and let their energy, their power washed over me. Again, I swam in the dark sea, drowning in the heavy, oily water, and glad about it.

This power, this delicious magic ... I needed it. I wanted it. It was made for me and belonged to me. Just me.

"If only she could see you now," someone muttered from behind me.

I opened my eyes and glanced over my shoulder. Bates stood in the doorway, his arms crossed, his eyes narrowed.

"What are you talking about?"

He took a step closer. "Delia and how she would be disappointed in how you just surrendered to the darkness."

I ...

Delia.

Who was Delia?

Oh my goodness.

Delia! I remembered Delia. She had been like a mother to me. She had taken me in when no one else did, she had helped me hide my magic, and she had given me a home of sorts. We had had our disagreements, but I knew she had loved me like a daughter.

I gasped, finally putting two and two together. When Delia told me about her time with Soren and Acalla, she mentioned that a warlock she fancied helped her escape.

Bates.

"It was you," I whispered. "You were in love with Delia. You helped her escape."

"That was a long time ago," he said, his voice quiet, low. "But I know she would have expected more from you."

I frowned, confused.

What was he talking about? Delia and her wishes, her expectations? Disappointment? Hundreds of thoughts swam through my mind, most of them warring against themselves.

A headache took hold of me.

I stared at Bates. "You're one of them. What do you care?"

He looked at me for a couple more seconds, then turned and left.

I stayed in that room, surrounded by the boxes and their immense power, that delicious darkness, that—

I shot to my feet and the piercing headache got worse as I ran to my bedroom. I slammed my door closed and leaned against it, breathing heavy as a sudden pressure strangled my lungs.

What the hell was going on?

Delia.

Boxes.

Darkness.

Power.

Want.

Need.

I made my way to my bed, sat on the edge, and pressed my fingertips to my temples, trying to ease my headache.

I felt like I was in a long, dark corridor, running for miles and miles, only now seeing a light in the distance, but it didn't matter how long and fast I ran toward it, it kept moving away from me.

I reached for the glass of water on the nightstand and my hand knocked something to the floor.

I picked up.

I froze.

The flower bracelet Killian had made for me.

Killian.

Oh, lord.

My chest constricted more and a sob rose to my throat.

Hundreds of thoughts and feelings overwhelmed me. The first time I saw Killian when I freed him from the box. The second time, when he killed all those demons and then collapsed on me. The few times he had almost kissed me, and then when he finally kissed me ... and promptly left me alone in the dark. How he had stopped my panic when the demon hunters locked us in a dark closet. That was when I first absorbed his box's magic; he had told me to. When he asked me to go to DuMoir Castle with him. That time when he lay over me in bed right before Tack invaded our bedroom at the inn. How he had fought for me when the Nightmist witches put me in a dark cell.

When he found me in my bedroom at DuMoir Castle, he told me he loved me, and then showed it when we made love.

A sob burst from me and tears streamed down my face.

Holy shit, what had I done?

I had let the boxes' powers take over me. I had allowed the darkness to control me. I had forgotten about Delia, about Killian, about everything that made me *me*.

Even now, I struggled with this knowledge. The boxes' power was too strong and I wasn't sure how long I could resist it. A few minutes? Maybe a couple of hours? I wasn't strong enough, not by myself.

I focused on my power, my Silverblood witch magic, that almost endless pool inside of me, and imbued the bracelet with a remembrance spell. I slipped it around my wrist and inhaled deeply, trying to calm myself down.

It was okay. I could work with this. Every time my mind slipped and I started to forget, the bracelet would act and send a jolt through me, reminding me of who I was and who I had left behind.

All right, I had my mind back. At least, for now.

But I wasn't sure if that was good or not. I was now conscious of all the shit I had done in the past few days—especially killing the higher demon. I had done it so easily, so cruelly, with so much pleasure ... it disgusted me.

I lay back in bed, hugged my pillow, and allowed myself to cry.

I had to get the disappointment and disgust with myself out of my system if I would find a way to fix this shit.

———

THE NEXT MORNING, the warlocks didn't call on me and I was grateful for that. I didn't know how I could act like a careless bitch so soon after breaking the darkness's hold over me. However, I didn't stay hunkered down in my bedroom all day either. I didn't have a plan per se, but I knew what my next step should be.

Right before lunch, I went to the library, where Bates often read.

Bingo.

Seated in one of the two leather armchairs by the window, Bates held a thick, leather-bound book, reading.

Suddenly nervous, I walked around the perimeter of the room, pretending to be looking at the books on the built-in shelves. What would I say to him? What if he had been baiting me?

"What I said worked, didn't it?" Bates asked in a low voice.

I froze. Slowly, I turned and looked at him. For a moment, I didn't do or say anything.

I nodded.

Bates dropped the book beside him and stood. He placed his hands inside his slack's pockets, glanced to the open door, and took a few steps closer.

"Why did you do it?" I asked, confused. "Aren't you one of them?"

Bates lowered his eyes for a second. "My heart hasn't been in it since Soren captured Delia and I fell for her. But once Delia ran with the boxes, I knew Soren wouldn't be able to finish the spell, and anything else he did would pale in comparison to that. Besides, I had nowhere to go."

"You could have found Delia, been with her."

He shook his head. "I would've drawn Soren to her. Even if I left, I couldn't go to Delia. But I heard about Delia and you, how close you were. And knowing Delia, I know she considered you like a daughter." He paused. "I can't let her daughter finish what she wanted to stop."

Daughter. A hand clutched my heart. I couldn't believe I had forgotten it, that I had let the darkness overshadow me. I touched the frail flower bracelet around my wrist and promised myself I wouldn't forget anymore.

As if teasing me, the call of the boxes intensified, and I closed my eyes, breathing in and out to push it back. Not today, Satan!

"But what can we do?" I asked, lowering my voice more. "The boxes are indestructible."

And there would be only Bates and me against a mansion of warlocks—I didn't think I had seen them all yet, but I had seen at least two dozen lurking around. If I tapped into the boxes' magic, I was sure I could at least hold them back while I escaped with the boxes, but I was also sure that if I did that, if I let the boxes' magic join mine again, I wouldn't be able to recover.

"I don't know," Bates muttered.

Footsteps approached. Bates rushed back to the armchair and picked up his book, and I turned to the nearest shelf and pretended to browse the stuffy volumes.

Tack and Damien entered the library. "There you both are," Tack said, annoyance in his tone. "Eldon wants us."

Without a spare glance, Tack and Damien left. Bates rose, dropped the book back in the seat, and walked out of the library as if we had never had this conversation.

I braced myself as I followed them. Each step I took put me closer to the boxes, and their call became louder and louder. I inhaled deeply and reached for my magic. It enveloped me, like an invisible layer over my skin, protecting me from the onslaught of power the boxes threw at me.

The boxes' power washed over me, pressing against my magical shield. I held my breath, reinforcing the light magic. It helped and it was slightly less uncomfortable.

Tack and Damien joined Eldon in the back of the room, while Bates glanced at me before doing so. He seemed worried. I was too. I wasn't a good actress, and I would have to pretend to be taken by the dark magic, careless, mindless, and under Eldon's thumb.

That didn't sit well with me.

I approached the warlocks, but was careful not to step into the circle. The boxes' allure intensified.

Eldon held up a thick black envelope. "This is an invitation to a ball."

Tack frowned. "Someone invited us to a ball? How did they even find us?"

"I didn't say it was our invitation," Eldon said with a grin. "Rosilla, the Witch Queen of the Bluemoon coven, is celebrating her one hundred and fiftieth birthday and invited supernaturals to attend her ball. I thought we could pay her a visit."

Damien snorted. "As much as I like to party, I think

everyone at that ball would attack us and kill us, as soon as we stepped foot in there."

"They can't." Eldon opened up the invitation. "It's written here that no weapon will be allowed inside and the place will be warded to neutralize or lessen everyone's power. Fights and public animosity are strictly forbidden. Everyone is supposed to leave their problems at the door or not come at all."

"So you're thinking of going to a ball we weren't invited to and mingling with our enemies?" Bates asked.

Eldon's smile lost its power. "Well, what a better opportunity to let the entire world know we're back and stronger than ever?"

"This is nuts," Tack said.

Damien's smile was as wicked as it got. "Free drinks, beautiful women, and enemies who can't kill us? I like it."

Eldon glanced at Bates. He shrugged. Eldon seemed almost annoyed with Bates, but then the expression passed. A dark glint shone in Eldon's eyes. "Then it's settled. We have a party to crash."

15

———

KILLIAN

Queen Rosilla was a good friend of Thea's, but to attend a freaking birthday ball right now? Twyla was missing and several vampires had been hurt during Lavinia's attack. Our boxes were gone and we still didn't have a clue where to go, how to proceed.

Celebrating anything seemed out of place.

Not to mention this was a witch queen's birthday. I was okay with Lavinia, Thea, Elisa, and Almae. I was also getting used to the idea of vampires and witches being so close together, and the Silverblood coven being so involved in DuMoir Castle business.

Another thing that still rubbed me wrong: going to a castle full of witches whom I used to hunt. Things had certainly changed in the last twenty years.

But Drake insisted. He said it was necessary if we wanted to keep the peace among the supernaturals.

"Besides, Almae had a vision," he told me the night before. "Eldon and the other warlocks will be there."

I frowned. "What about Lavinia?"

"She couldn't see Lavinia."

That was enough for me. If the warlocks who had kidnapped Lavinia and turned her into a dark witch would be there, so would I. On the way there, Drake repeated I couldn't under any circumstance start a fight, not even if I had a chance to kill Eldon and end this nightmare. If we did that, a bigger war could start and we were ill-equipped to deal with that.

"I can't promise you that," I said between gritted teeth.

"I know, but just … try."

That I could do. Maybe.

We arrived at the Bluemoon Estate—Drake, Thea, Keeran, Luana, Cain, Elisa, Zadkiel, Patrick, Shane, and I. The other princes stayed back to oversee the castle.

We were escorted to the side of the dark gray-blue stone castle, to a large stone porch between what looked like a cozy, but rather vast, sitting room with a hearth taller than I was, and a garden with blue flowers and stone paths and benches. With the sun setting, faint blue lights turned on, spread out through the place.

It was a beautiful setting, and I wished Lavinia was here with me to see it.

Lavinia …

I had to admit, after what happened a few nights ago, my feelings were conflicted. I loved her, she was my soulmate, and I knew she was under the warlocks' influence. However, it had been hard to see the destruction she left behind her, how she didn't seem to care. She had taken Twyla without a second thought.

She probably would have taken me too if Elisa and Zadkiel hadn't bumped into her.

The thought that I might have lost my soulmate was what I couldn't come to terms with. And I wouldn't. Not yet.

We joined the crowd, grabbed a table and drinks, and were formally introduced.

Queen Sarah of the Blackmarsh coven.

Queen Corvina of the Bonecrown coven and her second-in-command, Myra.

Queen Yira of the Wildthorn coven and her right hand, Neva.

I greeted Queen Denise of the Lightgrove coven again, along with two council members, Lenora and Grace, whom I had met with Lavinia when we visited the Light Castle in New Orleans.

I also met two interesting couples.

The first one was Wyatt and Farrah—a werewolf and a frost fae. Apparently, Farrah knew who Twyla was and had been contacted by Keeran and Luana to see her, but she couldn't until now.

And Twyla was gone.

"She's Prince Lark's sister," Farrah said to our circle. All of them seemed to know who that was. The beautiful fae with silver-blond hair turned to me. "He was a shadow fae prince who had been sent to Earth to oversee the fae here. He was greedy and evil."

Beside me, Shane stiffened. "Twyla doesn't seem like that."

"I don't know much about their history, but I heard they didn't get along well," Farrah said. She shook her head. "Wow, to know she has been stuck in that box for twenty years. That's crazy."

Oh, I knew about that.

Wyatt, the werewolf with hazel eyes, nodded. "You were in there too, right? I'm sorry you had to go through that, man."

"Thanks," I said, my voice tight.

Farrah and Wyatt struck up a conversation with Luana and Keeran. Drake and Thea joined in. The six of them seemed to know each other well.

The second couple I met didn't come alone. Rey Lowe, the headmaster of the Blackthorn Hunter Academy, and Erin Belmont, a young but already famous demon hunter, joined our group along with some of their friends and fellow demon hunters—Claire, Harper, Ava, and Harvey.

Wyatt and Farrah greeted Rey and Erin like old friends, and then introduced them to Shane and me.

"I'm sorry about Lavinia," Erin said. She was striking, with golden eyes and long black hair. "Thea asked us to come talk to her, and we were planning to, but then ... yeah. Sorry."

"We'll get her back," I told her, sure of that. Because it was the absolute truth. I wouldn't rest until I found a way to have my Lavinia back. "And then I'll be glad to introduce you to her. Almae told her that her witch side is a lot stronger than her demon hunter one, but I'm sure she would love to learn a little bit more about it anyway."

"We would be happy to give her a tour of the academy and the nearest Blackthorn Hunter outpost," Rey said. His eyes were silver, completely opposite to Erin's. They formed an impressive couple. "You too, of course."

I liked that idea.

Now, I had to come up with a plan to rescue Lavinia.

After that, Queen Rosilla stopped by our table and I was reintroduced to her. I had never met her officially, but I knew who she was. She remarked on how the vampires had hunted her coven, and how she'd even had some battles with Thea and the Silverblood witches, but it was all in the past, and she was glad we were able to come.

When she left to greet the other guests, Erin and Rey joined the conversation with the others, and Zadkiel took Elisa for a dance.

It was me, Shane, Patrick, and Cain. The four of us grabbed champagne flutes and stood beside our table, watching the crowd.

All the males were dressed in their finest suits and tuxedos, and the females donned their best gowns and hairdos. It all looked so fine and perfect under the blue lights.

Like a dream.

I missed my mate.

Patrick leaned closer and whispered, "Will you be able to control yourself when the warlocks make their entrance?"

My muscles coiled and my arm itched. Would I break the party rules if I punched him in the face?

"Why don't you mind your own business?" I asked.

"The warlocks and your evil soulmate are all of our businesses right now," he remarked. "If it depended on me, I would have killed her that night." I clenched my teeth, my fangs threatening to come out. "Then all of this would be over. But no, Drake didn't want to hurt her because of you." He scoffed. "What's one life when hundreds, maybe thousands of others are at stake?"

I turned to him.

Shane's arm shot between us. "That's enough."

"Shane is right," Cain said. He looked from me to Cain. "You two behave." He took a step closer. "And you, Patrick, stop being an ass."

Cain smoothed his tuxedo and turned—and bumped into a blonde woman wearing a long, dark green dress.

"Cain," she said, almost out of breath. "Hi."

"Norah," he said, almost nonchalantly. He looked at the red-haired woman by her side. "Doreen. How are you both doing this evening?"

"Late," Norah groaned.

"That's your fault," Doreen said. She put a hand over her mouth and fake-whispered, "Someone couldn't decide which dress to put on." She winked at Cain, then stepped past him.

Cain took Norah's hand and guided her to the porch, where the big open space created a dance floor. They joined the others who danced at the soft string melody.

Doreen sighed and grabbed a champagne flute from a passing waiter. She took a long sip and smiled at us. "Mission accomplished."

"Well done," Patrick said under his breath.

Doreen lifted a shoulder. "Now, I just stand here and watch."

"Or..." Shane started. From the little time I had spent with him, I had noticed Shane was a charmer, but when things got serious, he ripped that off as if it were a cloak he wore often, and focused. With a half-smile, he offered his hand to Doreen. "I could take you for a dance."

Doreen drank the rest of her champagne, handed the empty glass to Patrick, and slipped her hand into Shane's. The both of them strolled to the dance floor with the others.

"What the hell was that?"

Patrick shrugged. "Norah and Doreen are demon hunters. Norah is Cain's mate, though for some reason, she doesn't give in to Cain. At least, not completely."

I stared at him, baffled. Was that gossip? Coming from

Patrick? Wow ... "Sometimes you sound almost like a normal vampire."

Patrick glared at me. "I'm normal. And decent and I'm better than you'll ever be. If I can't stand scum and want to prune the weak links before they rust the rest of the chain, that's because I'm good at what I do, at what I am."

He dropped his and Doreen's glass on the table and walked away. I didn't care where he was going, or what he was up to, as long as he didn't bother me any longer.

I drank the rest of my champagne in one gulp.

Something tugged in my chest and I *knew*. I turned to the wide path where we had arrived from, and sure enough, there she was. A beautiful woman walking among four men. My throat dried at the sight of her. She wore an almost indecent bright red dress—one shoulder, cuts at the sides of her waist, showing skin, and a slit over her right leg that went up to her thigh. Her long, dark hair was pulled back by red gems and then flowed over her back in perfect waves, the red of the ends almost gone. Big silver earrings, a thick silver bracelet with red gems, and silver high heels completed her look.

My pants tightened instantly. But besides lust, I tensed. The four warlocks around her wore dark tuxedos and long capes over their shoulders—and I remembered them well. Eldon, Tack, Damien, and Bates. A surge of anger cut through me, taking my breath away, and it was all I could do not to rush to them and break their necks.

I wasn't the only one transfixed, watching as the five of them approached the party grounds. Everyone had stopped, including the supernaturals on the dance floor and the musicians playing the instruments. Queen Rosilla's face paled when she saw them, and along with a dozen witches, she rushed to meet them halfway.

Even though they spoke in hushed tones, most supernaturals here had great hearing, and we could make out most of their conversation.

"What are you doing here?" Queen Rosilla demanded.

Eldon showed her a black envelope. "We have an invitation."

"That wasn't for you."

"Can you prove that?" Eldon asked. He was provoking her. "Per your own rules, all supernaturals holding an invitation are welcome to this party, and there shall not be any arguments or fights while here." He pressed his hand over his heart. "You have my word, dear queen, that we'll behave if the others do. We're here to socialize."

Queen Rosilla bristled. "I find that hard to believe ... but I'll uphold my word. I'll let you and yours stay, but look wrong at any of my guests, and you'll be escorted out. And once you're off my estate, I can't guarantee your safety."

"That's perfect." Eldon bowed his head at her.

With a humph, Queen Rosilla marched away. She called for the musicians to play again, for the waiters to continue serving her guests, then she smiled at us and urged us to keep going as if nothing happened.

Right, because that was so damn easy.

Drake and Thea flanked me, along with the rest of our group, and all of us watched as Lavinia and the four warlocks walked the rest of the way and joined the party. My muscles tensed so hard, it was almost painful.

"Almae didn't see Lavinia in her vision," Thea whispered.

"We all know my mother's visions aren't one hundred percent accurate," Keeran added.

"Remember," Drake started, "no fighting, no arguments, no matter what. If you're feeling bold, try to trick them into saying more than they should. Otherwise, we behave." He paused and looked at Cain and Patrick. "Keep an eye on them. When they leave, you follow."

Cain and Patrick nodded.

"What about me?" I asked.

"You ... I know you won't pay attention to the warlocks," Drake said. Well, that was true. "If you approach her, be careful."

If.

There wasn't an *if* in that sentence.

I tugged at my tux's jacket and marched away from my group. Lavinia's eyes met mine, and for one brief moment, I saw them widen a millimeter or two, but that quickly went away. Disdain filled her features, but I could hear the rapid thump of her heart.

I walked toward her, but Eldon stepped in my way. "Oh, Killian, it's so nice to see you again."

"Don't provoke me, Eldon," I snarled. "I'm not here for you."

"I know." He stepped aside. "Don't try taking her from us. Or do. She'll kick your ass and run back to us anyway."

My jaw tight, I offered my hand to Lavinia.

She looked at it as if considering it. After three torturous seconds, she slipped her hand in mine. I didn't waste time and guided her to the dance floor, where most couples had resumed dancing, though now all their eyes were on us.

When we halted in the center of the dance floor, Lavinia turned to me. She twisted her hand in mine and placed her other one on my shoulder. I held my breath as I rested my hand on her bare waist.

It took me a few seconds, but finally, I started moving and

led her through the dance. I watched her beautiful face, her hazel eyes, her red lips ... Holy shit, being here, with her, and knowing she wasn't herself was damn hard.

I wanted to prod her to find out if there was a spark of light still in her. I had to know if I could still save her from this darkness. Again, no if. I would save her from it.

"You're awfully quiet," she said, her voice low. She knew most supernaturals here could hear us.

"I'm trying to come to terms that you're not the woman I love," I told her, as honest as I could.

She pursed her lips. "That must be hard."

"You have no idea."

"Can I tell you something?"

"Is it about where the boxes are, or how to take you back from the darkness?"

One corner of her lips came up. "Not really." She leaned closer to me. "But right now, it might be even better." I frowned. "Killian, look at my wrist." I did. Underneath the silver bracelet was the flower one I had given her when she had been at DuMoir Castle a few days ago.

I stared at her. "What ...?"

Lavinia pressed her body to mine and whispered in my ear so only I could hear it, "I broke through the darkness. I'm myself again."

I stilled. She had to tug me so I would keep dancing. "H-how can I be sure?"

She pulled back, looked at me, and shrugged. "I don't know. I have no proof. If only I could share with you what I'm feeling right now. Hatred for myself and everything I did while influenced by the darkness, shame for using you and stealing the boxes, and a crazy desire to kiss you right now."

Damn, when she said it like that.

I tightened my grip around her and walked from the dance floor, pulling her with me. We went through the wide-open doors leading to the sitting room and past it, into the castle. We passed a few supernaturals, mostly witches, but I ignored their wary gazes.

I found an empty office, dragged Lavinia in, and locked the door behind us.

She stood in the middle of the room, the desk behind her, while I paced two feet from her.

"Killian," she whispered. I halted. "I thought you would be happy, but it doesn't seem the case." She hugged herself. "You're scaring me."

I inhaled deeply. "I ... Lord, I'm holding myself back here, Lavinia, because all I want to do is to kiss you. I want to push those papers from that desk and take you right now, right here ... but damn, I won't make love to you if you're not you. I want to take your word, but you tricked me before."

"I know, and I'm so, so sorry." Tears filled her eyes. "I can never take back all that I've done. All the people I hurt. The ones that I killed." Her voice broke. "I hate myself for allowing the darkness to take me over so easily."

Shit. I stepped closer to her, my gaze on her face, on her trembling lips, on the gloss of unshed tears in her eyes. She was hurting so bad. A witch filled with darkness wouldn't be able to cry like this. I listened to her heartbeat, to how it spiked when I got closer to her. I remembered that hadn't happened a few days ago when she tricked me. I had been with her, hugged her, held her, and in no moment had she reacted this way to me.

I leaned into her, and her heart beat even faster. Her breath caught.

Holy shit.

I cupped her face and crashed into her. I closed my lips around hers, and she answered instantly. Holding on to my jacket, Lavinia parted her lips and let me take the kiss deeper, slower.

Damn, I had missed her.

True to my words, I pushed her back until her thighs hit the desk behind her, and helped her sit on it. Without breaking the kiss, I leaned her back, and with a big sweep of my arm, I pushed everything on the desk to the floor. Something made of glass broke, but I didn't care. I bent over her as I smoothed my hands up her legs, savoring her silky skin, and when I got to her thighs, Lavinia shivered. She clasped her hands around my shoulders, pulling me closer, as close as two dressed people could be.

As much as I would love to undress her, and myself, and take my damn time with her, we were in the middle of a party, and our enemies would be expecting us back soon.

Lavinia must have thought the same thing because she slid her hands down my chest and quickly worked on my pants—unbuttoning the waist and pulling down the zipper. She slipped her hand inside and stroked my hard-on.

I groaned and moved my lips to her neck. I couldn't help it, my fangs came out and I grazed them on her soft skin. It was all I could do not to bite her right there and then and taste her delicious blood. We couldn't risk having bite marks on her neck ...

She moaned when my teeth scraped her throat, and with her hand on me like that, I almost lost it.

I rained kisses down her collarbone and around the swell of her breast. Holy shit, how I wanted to strip her and enjoy her for eternity.

"I need you," Lavinia whispered. She pushed the waist of my pants down, just enough to free my hard-on, and she spread her legs wider.

Damn ... I brought my lips back to her as I smoothed her skirt to the side and snaked my hand to her inner thighs. I ran my hand over her core, and she shivered again. Doing this fast, not taking the time to pleasure her as she deserved, was killing me, but I needed her too. I tugged her panties to the side and pushed my hips to hers. Lavinia gasped against my mouth when I entered her, when I filled her. Damn, she felt so, so good. There wasn't anything better in this entire world. She had been made for me, there was no doubt of that.

The first two or three strokes, I went slow on purpose, enjoying the gentle friction. But shit, I wanted her so freaking much. I sped up, taking all she wanted to give me, going as deep and fast as I could. Lavinia slipped her hands under my shirt and jacket and grazed her nails on my back. This time, I shivered as the delicious sensation rolled up my spine.

"I love you," she whispered in my ear.

Holy shit ...

It was too much. I held on to her while I sped up even more, thrusting into her harder and deeper, and invoking little gasps and moans from her mouth. The delicious friction built up fast. Her walls tightened around me, her breathing hitched, and then her body trembled as the climax took over her. That was too much for me. A second later, I shattered. My body also shook as I came, and Lavinia wrapped her arms around me, holding me against her.

I rode down the climax, satisfied, but already thinking when I could have her again. This woman drove me crazy, in a good way. Despite our situation, she made me feel like I had never felt—satisfied, happy, complete.

I pulled back enough to look in her eyes. "I love you too."

She smiled at me, then captured my mouth with hers.

I sighed in the kiss, relieved she was here with me. The warlocks wouldn't touch her ever again.

16

LAVINIA

MY HEART HURT, BUT KILLIAN AND I COULDN'T WASTE TIME. I straightened my dress, and he pulled up his pants and smoothed his shirt, but all the while we were side by side, touching and kissing every few seconds.

I finally took three steps back. "Okay, if we continue like that, I won't be able to stop anymore, so ... yeah."

He smiled at me, so genuinely and so open, my heart squeezed. "That wouldn't be a bad thing."

No, it wouldn't. "If I stay out for too long, Eldon and the others will come after me."

Killian's smile faded. "How were they treating you? Have they hurt you? Have they ... hm, tried anything?"

I shook my head. "No, they haven't. They are mean, they like to insult and threaten me, but they know they need me to complete the spell. It's either me, or kidnapping Almae, which I don't think they want so ..."

"That's ... good. I guess."

"They injected me with a potion, though, something

unique that burns me from the inside when they willed it, which usually occurs when I defy them."

Killian's jaw tightened. "Is there a way to get rid of it?"

"As far as I know, it slowly fades from my system, so if they can't give me more, it should go away."

"Good. Now they will never have an opportunity to give it to you again."

"What do you mean?"

He stared at me. "Wait. You're coming with me, right? To DuMoir Castle?"

Oh. "No, I have to stay and—"

Killian cursed under his breath then stepped right in front of me. "Lavinia, you can't go back with them. Now that you're back to yourself, you can't go back. Like you said, they can't finish it without you or Almae. If you come with me, everything will be all right."

"I see your point." I reached over and adjusted his tie. "But if we think strategically, we could use this to our advantage. What other opportunity will you get to have a man on the inside? If I leave, then we lose access to the boxes they have."

He grasped my shoulders and rested his forehead on mine. "I don't like this."

I closed my hands around his biceps, loving I could feel his muscles even through the shirt and jacket. "I know. I don't either. Since I've woken up, I've been sick and worried. But so far, they haven't noticed anything." I pressed my lips before telling him, "Bates is helping me."

"Bates?" He pulled back and looked at me. His eyes widened as he remembered. "He's the one who loved Delia."

"Apparently, he still does." It was a beautiful, tragic love. I felt sorry for the both of them.

His eyes locked on mine, Killian cupped the nape of my neck with one hand. "I'm not sure I can let you walk away."

A small smile tugged on my lips. "You're the strongest man I know. I'm sure you can do it." Though, it did delight me that he felt that way about me. Truth be told, it would be damn hard to walk away from him now.

He exhaled. "All right, but if you're going, it'll be for a short period. We need a plan."

I looked to the floor, to all of the things Killian had hastily thrown to the side before he placed me on the desk. I picked up a closed ink bottle and a fountain pen. It was a modern one, with ink inside it, the same ink from the glass bottle.

"Keep this." I gave him the pen. "I'll find a way to weaken the warlocks, and when I do, I'll send you a message through the pen." I touched the bottle. "Then you come with the cavalry."

He took the pen and placed it in his pocket. "Where's their hideout?"

I shook my head. "I honestly don't know. We only come and go through portals. But I can ask Bates now. He'll tell me, and when I send you the message, I'll tell you that too."

"Sounds like a plan." Killian pulled me to him, embracing me tight. "I'll say it again, I don't like it."

I held on to him. "I don't either, but I'm trying to remind myself that it's almost over. We'll take down the warlocks, recover the boxes, find a way to destroy them, and then there will be nothing in our way. We can live in peace."

"And together." He buried his face on my neck. "I like that."

His lips brushed my skin, then his fangs. A shiver ran down my spine. I wanted him to bite me again, but we had no time. He dragged his mouth around my jaw and brought his lips to mine. He kissed me slowly and deeply, like he wanted to appreciate every second of it, commit it to memory, revel in the deliciousness of this moment.

"I love you so damn much," he whispered against my lips.

A pang cut through my heart. "I love you."

I let him kiss me for a few seconds longer, then I pushed him away. "All right. I have to leave." I extricated myself from him. He gave me a puppy look that had me second-guessing myself. "I'm serious. If I don't leave now, I won't ever leave, so ..." I pressed a peck on his lips and backed away fast.

Without looking back, I unlocked the door and left the office behind.

I left Killian behind, along with my heart in his hands.

I REJOINED THE PARTY, and as soon as I stepped out into the porch, Eldon and Tack surrounded me.

"Where were you?" Eldon asked in a hushed tone.

I kept my expression neutral, non-caring. "With Killian. He said he was trying to win me back." I looked around, disinterested. "I want some champagne."

Tack grabbed my arm. "We don't have time for that."

My will was to jerk my arm and yell at him, but I remained calm and careless. "Why? What happened?"

"The Dark Devils are here," Eldon told me.

Not so gently, Tack pulled me along with him as he and Eldon walked toward the path that led out of the estate.

"And we care because?" I asked.

"Because," Eldon rasped, "it doesn't matter. Let's go." He hurried his steps.

I dared glance back once, and saw Killian rejoined his group. My heart squeezed. I already missed him.

Eldon and Tack took me out of the party, through the expansive blue garden in front of the castle, to where Damien and Bates waited.

"Did Dommik see you?" Damien asked Eldon.

Eldon nodded. "Yes. Keep going." We walked faster to the edge of the property, where the ward against magic ended.

Once we were through, Eldon opened a portal.

Tack pushed me toward it. "Go."

I forced myself to not look back once more. Instead, I braced myself and entered the damn portal.

WHEN WE MADE BACK to the manor, Chess was waiting for Eldon at the front door.

"Report," Eldon told him as we entered the foyer.

"We apprehended two more supernaturals, my lord," Chess said, proud of himself.

My stomach sank. There were two more supernaturals in the basement, locked in those cold cells and waiting to be put in the boxes. Jeez, I had to find a way to weaken the warlocks fast, so Killian and the others could storm the castle.

"Which ones?" Tack asked.

"A goblin and a demon hunter," Chess said. "My contact is sure he found the dragon shifter but was unable to capture him."

Eldon nodded. "Send a dozen men to help him. That should be enough."

"Yes, my lord." Chess bowed his head low and left.

Damien yawned. "Since we couldn't stay long and enjoy the party, I'm going to bed."

"Me too," Bates said, heading for the stairs.

I stayed rooted in the foyer. "What happens now?" I asked, the words tumbling out of my mouth before I could stop them. The four warlocks turned to me. "We have several supernaturals, but not all the boxes. What's our next step?" I tried sounding like it didn't matter to me, but I wasn't sure I was fooling anyone.

"As a matter of fact, we'll be retrieving another box tomorrow," Eldon said. "So go rest. You'll need your strength."

He shooed me off, then headed up the stairs. Bates and I exchanged a brief, but tense look. The warlocks went to their bedrooms, and I forced myself to move and go to mine.

But sleep evaded me. Instead, I came up with a plan.

17

———

KILLIAN

WITH LAVINIA AND THE WARLOCKS GONE, AND THE ARRIVAL OF the Dark Devils, Drake decided it was time to leave before we started a real war in what was supposed to be a neutral place. Thea apologized to Queen Rosilla for our sudden exit, but as she had requested, we were trying to maintain the peace.

I didn't want to leave yet, but there was no other choice.

Back at Castle DuMoir, Drake called us to his office—Thea, Keeran, Luana, Almae, Shane, the other princes, and me.

"Tell them what you told me," Drake said. He stood behind his desk and chair, and he seemed more tired than usual.

I pushed away from the door, where I had been leaning, and walked closer to the desk and everyone else. "Lavinia broke through the spell. She's pretending she's still a mindless dummy, as best as she can, but it won't be long until they tell her to do something she doesn't want to do."

From the other side of the desk, Patrick humphed and crossed his arms. "How do you know she isn't playing you?

She might tell you she's not under their influence so you'll lower your guard."

Always him … "I think I know my mate."

"It didn't seem that way when she was visiting us a few days ago."

My hands closed into fists, I clenched my teeth, and took a step closer. Cain, who had been to my left, shot out a hand to stop me.

"When Killian found Lavinia in that place, in that state, we all believed she had gone through some major trauma," Thea said, her hands splayed on the chair's arms. "She had been quiet and reclusive, and Killian didn't think much of it, none of us did, quite frankly, because we thought she needed time to recover."

Almae nodded. "I examined her, and that's exactly what I thought."

Patrick shook his head. "That's still a crappy answer. It really doesn't seem like the two of you are mates."

This time, I advanced two steps before Cain stopped me.

Drake pointed a finger at him. "Patrick, if you're not going to say something helpful, then shut up!" I knew Drake was a little upset with Cain and Patrick, because despite their orders, the warlocks and Lavinia left too fast through a portal to track. There had been no way to follow them.

Patrick's jaw ticked, and he mumbled something under his breath, but we all chose to ignore him.

Thea was the one who spoke next. "Killian, please, continue."

"She gave me a pen." I showed them the fountain pen we had taken from the Bluemoon witches' castle. "She enchanted it and told me she would find a way to weaken the warlocks. When she did, she would send me a message through the pen. It'll magically write down where and when to attack."

"They won't be expecting that," Keeran said.

I nodded. "Exactly."

"That could work," Cain said. I stared at him for a second longer, remembering what I had learned about him during the party. He had a mate, a demon hunter, and they weren't actually together? I wondered why. "But we need to be ready."

"That's why I want you to prepare our vampires," Drake said. He looked at his mate. "Thea, can some witches come with us?"

"Of course," she promptly answered.

"I'll gather my warlocks," Keeran said.

"And I can spare some of my wolves," Luana added.

"Great." Drake pursed his lips. He was worried about this. "We'll get ready." He fixed his green eyes on me. "As soon as Lavinia sends her message, tell me."

I gave him one sharp nod.

We were dismissed. In a matter of seconds, all of us except Thea had left Drake's office. I walked out slowly, my attention on the pen in my hand. Shane caught up with me.

"I'm glad she's back to herself," he said. Shane had already shed his jacket and tie, and had opened up most of the buttons of his shirt. I knew that if depended on him, he would walk around in pants only ... but the first time he had done that, Drake had given him a friendly warning that this wasn't a wolf shifter pack, but a coven of refined vampires.

He had begrudgingly worn shirts ever since.

"Me too." I wasn't only glad, I was relieved. I'd thought I would have a lot of work ahead of me to bring her back to me. "Though she's upset about what she has done."

Shane nodded. "I bet."

Laughter echoed behind us. "And you bought that?" I stilled and Shane shot me a look. "Are you that stupid? I would bet my fortune she's still playing you."

"Patrick ..." Gritting my teeth, I turned and faced him. "Walk away before I break your nose."

Shane's lips curled up. "No, don't. I would like to see that. You know what? I would join in and break your jaw too."

Patrick glared at both of us. "You'll send us directly into a trap, and once Drake sees that, he'll remember I warned him about it. He'll demote you."

I took a step toward Patrick. This time, Shane didn't stop me, and Cain wasn't here to do it either.

I exhaled through my nose and tried to calm down—try was the key word here. "You're not worth my time."

Acting like the bigger man, I walked away.

From my back, I could hear Shane's snicker and Patrick's annoyed grunt.

Point for me.

LAVINIA

THE NEXT MORNING, ELDON CALLED FOR ME. SINCE HE HAD told me we were going after a box, I dressed in leggings, a long sleeve tee, and boots. If we were going somewhere cold, well, I hoped he had another thick coat for me.

I stopped in the kitchen on my way to the summoning room, where I grabbed a cup of coffee and a bagel for breakfast. I was giving myself more time to calm down, refocus, play pretend. My stomach was in knots at the thought of finding another box. I mean, Killian and I had mentioned finding them all before, but that had been different. We wanted to destroy them. I didn't like finding the boxes for these warlocks.

But right now, I had no other option.

I drank my coffee and ate half of my bagel before walking toward the summoning room. I shoved the last piece in my mouth as I stepped into the room.

Eldon, Tack, Damien, and Bates were already there, as usual, as were the seven boxes in their places in the circle. Their power hit me right away—it never really went away, but whenever I got too close, it was like the air scorched, and I could barely breathe.

"Where are we going?" I asked, once again forcing my voice to sound bored.

"I'll show you." Eldon beckoned me closer.

Like a good puppy, I did as he asked. I walked to him, but when I skirted the circle, a force hit me in the side. I yelped and stepped into the circle. The magic of the boxes pressed against me and I felt dizzy.

Then that forsaken burning pain spread over every inch of my body, and I crouched down, gasping for air.

Eldon moved his hand, and the pain increased.

"My, oh my, dear Lavinia."

"W-what are you doing?" I asked, my voice barely above a whisper. It hurt to talk.

He shook his head. "I didn't think you were so naive."

Shit, shit, shit. This could only mean one thing. "What the hell are you talking about?"

The pain increased and I screamed.

Tack walked closer, but like Eldon, he didn't come into the circle. "You thought we wouldn't find out?"

Damien stepped to his side. "You broke free of the magic and talked to your sweetheart. What did you tell him?"

I blinked. Oh, shit. "I don't know what you're talking about!"

Tack groaned. "You're making this harder."

Damien's lips curled up. "I like it."

Despite myself, I glanced at Bates. He stayed several steps back, quiet as ever, and this time avoiding my gaze.

Eldon walked the circle's perimeter. "We can go about this the easy way, or the hard way." He glanced at Damien. "If she resists, I'll let you play with her."

Damien licked his lips.

My stomach curled. Oh, lord.

"Answer the question," Tack said.

I shook my head. The pain was so intense, I didn't remember anything anymore. "What question?"

"What did you tell Killian?" Eldon asked. "Did you tell him where we are?"

I clamped my mouth, closed my eyes, and breathed in. I focused on my chest moving up and down, slowing my breathing, pushing away the pain. I wouldn't surrender so easily.

"Can I play with her now?" Damien asked, sounding like a kid asking for a lollipop after dinner.

Eldon didn't answer. Instead, he twisted his hand again, and along with the incredible pain, a dark bolt flew to me. I pushed back on my heels, but something bumped behind my legs. The bolt hit me square in the chest, and I fell seated on a chair. Magical ropes snaked around my legs and wrists, forcing my arms apart and to the side of the chair.

I screamed. "What the hell?"

Eldon picked up a box from one of the points inside the circle, walked in the circle, and approached me. "I'm afraid we'll have to start all over again."

I gaped at the box in his hand. Oh, God, no. I pressed my lips together. I wouldn't tell him about anything, no matter what he did.

The ropes tightened around my wrists and moved my arm up. I screamed, trying to regain control of my movement, but I couldn't. There was nothing I could do.

Eldon pressed the box against my hand.

And the box's magic flooded into me like an avalanche.

I BLINKED AND LOOKED AROUND. Why was I tied to this chair?

"Lavinia?" Eldon asked. I looked at him. "Who's your master?"

"You are, my lord," I answered.

He smiled at me. The magical ropes disappeared from around my wrists and legs. Completely sore, I pushed up from the chair. What had happened to me?

It didn't matter, not when I could see all my beloved boxes in the circle, when I could feel their magic attuned to mine, when I could bring it inside me, fill my veins with its delicious power.

I inhaled deeply, filling my lungs with their dark power too.

"Lavinia," Eldon started. "You met with Killian last night. What did you tell him?"

I cocked my head and thought for a bit. I met with Killian? It took me a moment, but I remembered. I frowned, not understanding my past actions. "I gave him a pen. I told him I would send him a message through the pen when I had weakened you." I fished the bottle of ink from my pocket. "I was going to use this."

Eldon grabbed the bottle from me. "Good girl." He examined the bottle. "Today, we'll find the new box. I think its power will give us an advantage. But when we're back ... Tack, assemble our warlocks, get them ready. In two days' time, we send a message to Killian. We let them come."

"Into a trap," Damien said, hunger in his voice.

I liked it.

Eldon grinned.

Chess rushed into the room. "Sorry to interrupt, my lord, but you have to see this."

Eldon and the others hardened right away. They followed Tack out, and I went with them. We halted at the mansion's entrance, where from the front porch, we could see a large group marching toward us from the distance.

"Is that DuMoir vampires?" Tack asked.

A moment later, Eldon said, "No. It's the Dark Devils."

Damien cursed. "They found out about the boxes. They came for them."

"How did they find us?" Bates asked.

"It doesn't matter," Eldon said. "Tack, call the warlocks now. We have a battle to fight. And win." Tack ran into the mansion, with Damien and Bates at his heels. Eldon turned to me. "Lavinia, absorb the boxes' magic. As much as you can. And then ... kill them all."

19

KILLIAN

I KNEW LAVINIA'S MESSAGE WOULDN'T COME RIGHT AWAY. IT even might take her a few days, or a full week, or longer, to set it all up. She had to pretend to be still consumed by darkness while plotting how to weaken the warlocks. Not just plotting but executing it as well.

I paced the space in front of my bed and groaned. I hated the idea of her alone in a nest of snakes. I knew she was capable of taking care of herself, but that didn't mean I didn't want to help. I wanted to be there with her, for her, forever.

Staying back and waiting was the worst.

As the days passed, my apprehension grew. Shane tried telling me what I first told myself. That she had to be so careful, it would take a while for her to set everything up. Patrick kept getting on my nerves by saying Lavinia was playing me again. She wasn't getting ready to send us a message to attack the warlocks. She was getting ready to attack us while we were distracted.

I wanted to punch him so damn hard.

His words didn't affect me. I knew in my heart, that this

time, Lavinia wasn't lying. She was herself again, and soon she would send me the damn message.

Because I wanted to be ready for the upcoming battle, I fed twice a day. Sometimes Shane went with me, though he ran far from me when I was in true hunting mode. Not because he was afraid I would attack him, but because he didn't want to see me kill innocent deer—his words, not mine.

At this point, DuMoir Castle wasn't in lockdown anymore, but we still hadn't found who had helped the warlocks kidnap Lavinia. So far, our theories were that it had been another clueless vampire like Ballein, who did it in exchange for something they desired, or that one of the warlocks had sneaked into the castle and kidnapped her.

None seemed good, though.

I sighed and went to my window. The sun was high in the sky, shining down on this world as if it was the most perfect thing to exist. Down below, vampires, witches, warlocks, and Starlight wolves had gathered, some of them training, some talking and mingling—but all of them waiting for the damn message that never came.

As if I had willed it, the pen in my pocket jolted.

Holding my breath, I picked it up and went to one of my nightstands, where I had left some paper ready. I gently pressed the tip of the pen to the paper ... and the pen moved of its own accord. All I had to do was hold it upright.

A sequence of numbers appeared first, followed by a short message.

We don't have much time.

—Lav

I picked up the paper and ran to Drake's office. I burst

into the room, obviously interrupting an important talk between him and Cain.

"I've got it." I lifted the paper. "Lavinia sent us coordinates."

THANKFULLY, we had powerful witches and warlocks in our midst—never thought I would say that—and when the sun began to set, they opened portals to the location—a remote wooded area in South Dakota. We portaled just outside the coordinates range, where the snow covered the ground and most of the naked tree branches. Once again, the witches and warlocks stepped up by revealing the hidden road that led deeper into the woods.

And then, a mile out, we heard the sound of battle.

"What is that?" Drake asked. He had taken the lead.

I focused on the noises. "It's a fight." But that didn't make sense. Even if Lavinia had been found out, it would be her against all other warlocks. By the grunts, clanks, and other sounds we heard, it was obvious there were two large groups fighting each other.

We approached with care, trudging through the snow, until the manor and the battle came into view. The gray manor looked like an old, abandoned boarding school, with its severity and creepiness factor high on my scale.

And around it, vampires fought against warlocks.

"The Dark Devils," Cain said through gritted teeth.

"How did they find the warlocks here?" I asked.

"That doesn't matter," Drake answered. He turned to the rest of our big party. "We are going in there and stopping them, even if it means killing them all. Just spare Lavinia and any other innocents who are clearly trapped there. Clear?" The message was passed through the crowd, and we all nodded. He pumped his fist in the air. "Attack!"

We ran from our hiding place and joined the fray.

Both the Dark Devils and the warlocks were surprised to see us there, but they quickly changed tactics and attacked us too. Three enemy groups fighting each other—this wouldn't end well.

I made my way through the vampires, approaching the house and the vampires, my eyes moving side to side, searching for Lavinia. Where was she?

Han, one of Dommik's favorites, stepped in my way, and I moved to the side, wrapped my arm around his shoulders, and broke his neck. His body fell at my feet and I stepped over it, finally reaching the manor's front stairs.

Just as Lavinia walked out, two vampires dangling in midair from their feet beside her. She lifted her hands and the vampires floated higher in the air. She swept her hand to the side as if she was wielding a sword. The vampires screamed for half a second before their heads fell to the ground and rolled toward me.

I stared at Lavinia.

At the wicked smile on her lips.

At the dark glint in her eyes.

She let the bodies drop to the ground like rotted potato sacks.

"Lavinia," I whispered, stunned.

No, it couldn't be.

The darkness had gotten her again.

Or had she played me?

She fixed her gaze on me and her smile widened. "Finally, you're here."

20

LAVINIA

I KNEW THE VAMPIRE BEFORE ME. I STARED AT HIM, A FIERCE smile on my lips, while my mind and my heart screamed at each other.

Where had I seen this vampire before? Why did he matter?

"Kill him, Lavinia!" Tack ordered from inside the house.

I called my magic and faced the vampire. I would kill him in two seconds, and then move on to the next one. I raised my hands to throw my magic at him.

"Your bracelet," he said.

I blinked, my magic flickering. "What?"

"Look at your wrist."

Despite myself, I did. I looked at my wrist. A flower bracelet wrapped around my wrist, a frail thing that would shrivel and break.

An image made its way to my mind.

This vampire—Killian—slipping the bracelet over my hand while looking at me with loving, adoring eyes.

Then another.

Killian pushing me to the desk at the Bluemoon witches' estate and kissing me ... gliding his hands up my legs, while I reached under his pants. My body lit with an intense need and love grabbed me by the throat.

I gasped, as if I was drowning and needed to get as much air as I could before sinking again.

I sank again.

Darkness fell over my eyes.

This vampire had to die. Tack had said so.

A warlock appeared in front of me. "Lavinia, stop."

Bates. Another one of my masters. I stopped.

He grabbed my arm and pulled me to the side, behind a thick pillar, hidden from the fight around us. The vampire followed us.

"What happened?" the vampire said, his voice grave, agitated.

"Eldon found out she had broken through the darkness," Bates said in a clipped tone.

Right. The darkness. The same one wrapped around me right now, squeezing my chest, making it hard to breathe. It wanted more. More energy, more power, more life.

I gasped, once more fighting against the dark tide forcing me down.

"He forced the boxes on her again," the vampire said. Killian. That was his name ... and there was more I wasn't remembering. That the darkness didn't let me remember. Bates nodded. "How did she send the message, then?"

"I did," Bates said. "Eldon asked me to do it, but I thought it was better if you came. Otherwise, Lavinia would have killed them all and then she would be lost forever."

I tried focusing on their words, but they had little sense to me.

A vampire ran past us toward the house's front door, and I got ready to blast him to hell. Killian lowered my arm before I could even call my magic.

"Fight the darkness, Lavinia." He didn't let go of my arm. Instead, he stepped closer and cupped my face with his other hand. "You've done it before. You can do it again."

I shook my head, my thoughts lost in a dark tunnel.

Fingers poked my collarbone, hard and powerful, and magic shot through me. Bates's magic washed through me like sunshine dragging away the darkness. I gasped once more. The magic wasn't strong and the darkness started advancing again. But this time, I grabbed on to this foreign magic, and to my own. I held on to Killian's hand as hard as I held on to the light inside me. I pushed the boxes' magic away, inch by inch, slowly and painfully. I gritted my teeth and groaned as if I was ripping my own soul from inside me.

Then, it was gone.

The darkness left me.

I took in a deep, clean breath. I felt the darkness surrounding me, trying to push through the bubble I had built around myself. No, it wasn't getting back in. Especially now that I had Killian here with me.

I looked at him, tears in my eyes. "I'm sorry I wasn't strong enough."

He leaned into me and pressed his forehead to mine. "Don't say that. You're one of the strongest people I know. You just broke through the boxes' magic a second time. That's amazing. You're amazing."

I sighed, wishing I could melt into him and pretend nothing else was happening right now.

"We don't have time for this." Bates grabbed my arm. "We need to get to the boxes. You need to take them."

Reluctantly, I disentangled myself from Killian, but he didn't let go of my hand. I nodded to Bates and he started toward the manor. Killian and I followed him. The fighting went on around us, but we dodged it as best as we could. When someone attacked us directly, Killian used his super speed and strength to shove the vampire or warlock far away.

We halted before the last hallway leading to the summoning room—warlocks crammed the space, all ready for a good fight.

"Shit," I muttered.

"Lower your guard," Bates ordered them.

The warlocks only raised their hands, dark globes of magic hovering over their open palms.

Chess stepped forward. "We don't take orders from you anymore."

Too quick for me to make sense of it, someone appeared from behind Bates. Bates groaned and fell to his knees. I stared at Tack, at the blood-stained dagger in his hand.

What ...?

Tack came for me next, and in my shocked state, I barely had time to react. But Killian did. With his fangs showing and the black lines around his eyes, he grabbed Tack by the throat. Tack was ready, though. He threw a powerful magic bolt at Killian's chest. Killian let go of Tack and jerked back.

I turned to Tack, my hands up and the magic gathering at my fingertips. But he ran behind Chess, and the warlocks threw bolts at us.

Killian hooked a hand around Bates's elbow and we ran for cover around an archway. Killian gently leaned Bates against the wall and I crouched beside him.

"You're going to be okay," I whispered, thinking of Delia and him. He had helped her escape, at the risk of being found out. And now he had helped me, and that had cost him.

"Liar," he croaked. A cough rose beyond his tongue and red stained his lips. He fixed his glassy eyes on me. "I'll tell Delia she should be proud of you."

My breath caught. Holy shit. I opened my mouth to tell him he would have time to tell her that later, but I heard as he sucked in one last breath, and then his chest stopped.

I glanced at Killian. He shook his head. "Tack pierced his heart from behind. There was nothing we could have done."

A lump formed in my throat, but I swallowed it. This wasn't the time for being sentimental. We had to get to the boxes, even if I hated the idea of being near them. We had to get them from Eldon and the others and take them somewhere safe, where we could find out how to destroy them.

A vampire and a warlock fought each other and fell right at our side. They didn't even pay attention to us, but that was a sign. "We need to move."

"As much as I think the both of us are powerful, I'm not sure we can take on twenty warlocks by ourselves," Killian observed.

I knew that, but what other choice did we have?

"We can help," a new voice said.

I turned around and saw Shane in loose shorts. Behind him, Drake, Thea, and many others fought against other vampires and warlocks. They quickly cleared the hallway behind us ... now we needed to clear the one in front of us.

One vampire advanced on Drake.

"That's Dommik," Killian said. I knew that but only because I had almost killed him a few minutes ago. Eldon had ordered me to hunt him down. I was on my way to him when Killian found me.

And helped me break free.

Six other vampires followed Dommik, but Drake was well equipped with not only his power, but with Thea and a few others I didn't recognize.

Killian turned to Shane. "What happened to your clothes?"

He shrugged. "Already shifted and back. Brought plenty of extra pants and shorts just in case." His gaze found the body beside us, then he spied out the archway. A black bolt zipped through the air, missing him by less than an inch. "Crap. Are you two ready?"

No. Not really. But we would never be ready. I nodded; Killian rolled his neck.

Shane looked over his shoulder and whistled. In five seconds, Cain, Patrick, Elisa, and Zadkiel broke from the other fight and joined us. Now we were six against twenty-ish. Not perfect but better odds, for sure.

Shane shifted into his wolf form, ripping through his shorts, and lunged at the warlocks. The rest of us ran after him. Two witches, a vampire, a wolf shifter, and an angel. Quite the group.

Besides the numbers, the warlocks had an advantage of being in a narrow hallway. To really make a difference, we rammed into them, pushing them back and forcing them to scramble.

Killian and Shane took the lead while Zadkiel worked the middle. Elisa and I stayed back, throwing bolts of magic at warlocks who tried to escape or attacked our friends from behind.

To my surprise, in less than ten minutes the hallway was clear and we reached the summoning room.

I tried the door and groaned. "Of course it's locked." I

placed my hand over the knob and sent my magic to it, but before it could wrap around the bolt, Shane rammed into the door, breaking it open.

Inside, Eldon, Tack, and Damien stood inside the circle, the seven boxes in their places. Eldon chanted lowly while Tack and Damien looked out at us.

Shane jumped at them, but bounced back with a yelp.

"They activated the circle," Elisa said.

"I think I can break it," I said. I crouched down, touching the circle's outer lines. Power rushed through me, the circle and the boxes attuned to me. Even if Eldon could use it, he didn't have the same affinity.

The boxes' power brushed against my skin, alluring and promising. A delicious temptation I didn't understand why I had to resist. I shook my head and focused.

I pushed my magic into the circle. It hummed loudly, dampening the dark magic. Eldon sped up his chanting, and Tack and Damien tried kicking me away, but Killian and Shane came to my side. Each time one reached for me, Killian tried grabbing their hands or feet, and Shane tried biting them.

A loud zap went through the circle when I broke it. I fell back, suddenly exhausted. Before I could recover, Killian, Shane, Elisa, and Zad rushed into the circle and subdued the warlocks.

I reached for one of the cloaks in the corner of the room and made my way to the boxes. I wrapped three in one cloak, then reached for another one.

Just then, more people ran into the room—Drake, Thea, Dommik, Patrick, Cain, and some other vampires.

It was pure chaos.

While twisting out of Drake's way, Dommik's eyes landed

on the boxes. He dodged out of the fight and came at me. I conjured blue bolts to throw at him, but before I could do anything, Killian stepped in my way, meeting Dommik halfway. The two of them exchanged punches and kicks, while Drake and the others got busy with Dommik's vampires.

Eldon, Tack, and Damien joined us, coming directly for me. I threw out a shield in front of myself, but their assaults were strong and frequent. After breaking the circle's power, it took everything in me to keep the shield up.

I groaned with the effort, my arms trembling.

My shield shuttered and broke, and I tried to accept that this was for the best. Hiding behind a shield didn't win wars. I threw my bolts at them as fast and hard as I could, while dodging theirs. Tack threw a big one that forced me to retreat several steps. Eldon dove for the cloak with the boxes.

"No!" I screamed.

Killian immediately turned his back to Dommik and went for Eldon. Tack and Damien pressed harder, keeping me from stopping Eldon.

Killian rammed into Eldon and went directly for the throat. The two fell on the floor, and Killian sank his teeth into Eldon's neck. Eldon screamed.

Wiping at his mouth, Killian shot up and turned to Tack and Damien.

I looked at the boxes in the cloak, to make sure they were safe, only to find they were gone. Despair filled my chest as I scanned the room. At the doorway, Dommik held the cloak and the boxes tight. He glanced back at his vampires, but didn't say anything, didn't warn he was leaving. He was sneaking out of the room, and no one saw it.

"Dommik!" I screamed. "He's getting away with the boxes!"

That got the room's attention. Dommik shot me a death glare before dashing away from the room in his vampire speed. Killian made for him, but Tack and Damien kept him busy. Drake, Thea, and the others tried going after him too, but Dommik's vampires stayed in the way.

After a few seconds, I realized that even if I were to go after him, it was too late. By now, Dommik would be a couple of miles down the road. I had no chance of catching up with him. Almost no one had.

Three boxes were gone.

Renewed with frustration, I faced Tack and Damien with Killian. Both of them moved their hands, as they had done before, accessing the potion inside of me. But all I felt was a trickle of pain, something easy to ignore. Realizing what happened, they stared at me for a moment, dumbfounded. Then they acted. Tack and Damien threw magic after magic at us, but Killian dodged them, and I threw my bolts at them, breaking their focus. Killian took advantage and tackled Damien. He wrapped his arms around Damien's head and snapped his neck.

Eyes wild, Tack brought up a shield between us. Then he opened up a portal.

"No!" I shouted. One second, he was here. The next, he was gone and the portal was closed. "Shit," I muttered.

"It's okay," Killian told me. "He won't do much damage by himself."

True. And thankfully, he hadn't taken any of the boxes with him. I glanced at the scene around us—the fighting was dying out as Drake, Thea, and the others overpowered the vampires and warlocks and killed most of them.

Killian stepped into me and pulled me into a bear hug. I

melted into him, suddenly so tired. "It's over," he whispered into my hair.

"This battle, yes, but Dommik got away with three boxes."

"We'll destroy the four boxes left, and the prototype. He won't be able to complete the spell with just those. It's over," he repeated. I nodded, my chin rubbing his shirt.

I wanted to stay with him like this forever—well, maybe after a shower, some food and rest, then yeah. Like this forever.

I reluctantly stepped back from his embrace. "We should gather the boxes."

Killian nodded. "Right."

I grabbed another cloak from the corner and Killian went for the prototype on the long table along the back wall. I laid down the cloak in the center of the circle, a couple of feet from Eldon's body. I wrinkled my nose. With the corner of the cloak, I reached for the first box.

A hand closed around my wrist. "You bitch!"

I screamed. Eldon rolled to his side, blood seeping from his open wound, and reached for the box.

I groaned, trying to break free from his grip, but I was still in shock. He hadn't died? Eldon grabbed the box and pressed it against my hand. The ridges in the box's smooth surface appeared, the light shone bright. The box shook hard and opened.

Smoke swirled around us.

"Good bye, bitch." Eldon pushed me into the box.

21

KILLIAN

I HEARD LAVINIA'S SCREAM.

I dropped the prototype on the floor. I ran to her.

But I was too late.

She disappeared into the smoke.

Rage surged in every cell of my body.

I didn't think.

I grabbed Eldon's shoulders and dove into the box before it closed.

We landed hard on the rough ground, me on top of Eldon. I knew the bastard was bleeding out, but I didn't care. I needed to burn away the pent-up rage. I wrapped my legs around his waist and pulled on his head.

It came off in a bath of blood and gore.

I dropped the head, wiped my hands on his shirt, and stood.

I looked around and a wave of despair hit me hard in the chest. Dark skies, heavy clouds, thick lightning, loud thunder, dry air, warm breeze, no landscape other than the desert ground for miles and miles and miles.

Shit, I couldn't believe I was back here.

And Lavinia was here somewhere too. I glanced around again. Hadn't she come through a few seconds before me? Where was she? I let out a sigh. This place was treacherous and unpredictable. In my time here—which hadn't felt like twenty years and made me think time passed differently here —I couldn't make sense of it. I would have drawn a map, if I had found a pen and paper, but even if I had noted down everywhere I had been, I believed the landscape, the land per se, was always changing, moving, as if it was fluid and fickle.

But the worst part was the monsters. This land was filled with nasty monsters I had never seen or heard of before. At some point, I had believed I was in a bad part of the under-world and these were demons. That I had died and my soul was so tainted I had to pay for it, and the demons were my punishers. But with time I learned this was another realm and the creatures here were unlike anything else.

I had never seen another earthly supernatural or human in here before, but now that I knew about the boxes, I was sure the other supernaturals who inhabited their boxes were somewhere in here too. I promised myself to come back later and search for them, free them from their boxes, even if we couldn't destroy them. At least, that was what I had hoped someone would have done for me.

But for now, I would find Lavinia.

With a long exhale, I started moving.

The majority of the monsters here didn't have rhyme or reason, but there was one group, one powerful enough group, who ruled a corner of this world and thought they could and should rule everything.

If someone knew where Lavinia was, it was them.

I rolled my shoulders, focused on my surroundings in case random monsters showed up and attacked me—that happened a lot here.

22

LAVINIA

I HID BEHIND A LONELY ROCK IN THIS FORSAKEN, DESERT LAND, and held my breath. Several yards from the rock, a creature with bluish skin sniffed the air.

I pressed a hand to my mouth to keep from yelping, or even breathing too loud. The other hand pressed to the side of my head, where a small bump had formed. I believed I had hit my head and fainted when I entered the box. When I came to, I was in a dark, dry, desert land. At first, I panicked because of the darkness, but this place was open and never ending. The dark part still got to me, but the lightning and thunder came frequent enough—and it scared the hell out of me—that it illuminated the place some.

As soon as I arrived, I looked back and couldn't see any portals or doors. There was no way for me to go back. I stood my ground for a while, hoping a hand would reach out from the air and bring me back to the warlocks' manor.

But seconds turned into minutes, and minutes ... well, I lost track of time. And I was fairly sure time here was different. It certainly felt like it, and after seeing Killian's shock when he learned twenty years had gone by while he was in here ... yeah, it confirmed that theory.

Then, the creature appeared in the distance and I ran in the opposite direction. Thankfully, a large rock stood out like a sore thumb in the empty landscape, and I hid behind it. I hoped the creature hadn't seen me, but now that it was sniffing the air, I thought it had at least caught my scent.

I also hoped the creature was dumb enough not to come looking for me in the only place to hide nearby.

I heard the shuffle of slow footsteps. My heartbeat sped up, painfully hammering against my rib cage. Holy shit ...

Even through my fear, my curiosity still rang loud. I carefully spied out from behind the rock—the creature had gooey, bluish skin with random patches of dark fur. Its limbs were long and thick, and its feet and hands looked more like sharp claws. Its head was abnormally big; the muzzle was longer than a wolf's and its teeth seemed larger, stronger. Its eyes were red and I couldn't see any ears, only two horns that curled behind its head, probably balancing its weight.

I had never seen anything like it, and I truly hoped this one was the only creature like this in this place. But the many scars on Killian's arms, back, and chest told me otherwise.

Shit, I had to find a way out of here.

The creature stopped and I recoiled behind the rock again.

After a while, the footsteps started again and grew distant. I waited behind the rock, trying to slow my heartbeat now that the danger seemed to be getting away.

I waited a while longer, and then spied around the rock. There were no more creatures around. With a relieved sigh, I stood up.

And something rammed into my back, taking me down

to the hard, rough ground. I yelled as the creature snapped its teeth at my throat. I called my magic and wrapped it around myself like armor. The creature tried to bite again, but its muzzle bounced back against my improvised shield. I took advantage of that and rolled off the creature and scurried to my feet. The creature shot up too and came at me again.

I threw out the biggest blue bolt I had ever conjured. It hit the creature's head and jolted its entire body. It fell back with a deafening thud.

I stood still for a minute, trying to slow down my heart once again, and to make sure the damn creature wouldn't get up again.

Then, I collapsed on my knees.

Holy shit, after the battle at the warlocks' manor, this last bolt had drained me way too much. I needed to rest for a bit. I also needed some fuel—a.k.a. food and water—but I doubted I would easily find anything here.

I frowned. How had Killian survived?

I glanced at the creature's body. Oh, shit. Ew!

Well, my diet was different from Killian's.

Angling my body so I wouldn't see the dead creature, I leaned against the rock and took deep breaths. Even if I couldn't eat anything, a little rest would do me good and recharge my magic. It seemed I would need it while in here.

My heart squeezed.

Killian had been trapped in here for twenty years. How long would I be? No, I couldn't think like that. No one knew what had happened to Killian other than the people who had done this to him. My case was different. Killian had seen me, and I was sure others around us figured it out too. He and the others were probably trying to open the box again to get me out. Shit, Almae hadn't gone to the battle, but it was okay. Killian would take the box to her, she would open it, and I would be free.

All I had to do was wait. From what I understood, the box's portal didn't open in the same place, but I didn't feel like wandering in an unknown land, not even for food.

So, I crossed my legs, lay my head back on the hard rock, closed my eyes, and forced myself to not despair. Killian would come for me soon.

I stilled my breathing and tried to clear my mind, like I was meditating.

In a strange land plunged in darkness and full of hungry creatures.

Great.

I opened my eyes again and let out a long exhale.

This wasn't working. I had to do something. But what? Walk around carefully and try to find some help? Or maybe the other supernaturals who were trapped in this place. Because it was the same place for all the boxes, right? I wondered if Soren and Almae knew what they were doing, where they were sending the supernaturals ... It didn't matter. Right now, my best chance to survive this place was to go searching for Twyla and the others who were trapped in here.

I stood from my hiding place.

Someone jumped on me—no, not someone, and not just one. Five ugly creatures crowded me, their big, clawed hands scratching my skin when they held me tight.

I screamed and pulled against their hold. Then, I shut my mouth and called on my magic. I would blast these damn creatures to hell and—

Everything went black.

I WOKE up with a start and almost yelled when I faced the creature carrying me in his thick arms. I also almost fainted again with the piercing pain that came from the back of my skull. I tried reaching for it, but besides being almost crushed in the creature's arms, I was bound by some kind of rope around my wrists and ankles. Though, I felt something wet at my nape. Whatever the monsters used to hit me had done some damage, but not enough to kill me.

If the creature had noticed I woke up, it didn't show me. It just kept staring ahead and I followed its gaze—just the same dark desert landscape from before.

Where were they taking me?

I dared a glance up at my captor. This creature had a red tint to his dark, scaly skin. It had four arms, and was as big as a bull on the lower body. I looked at the others. They were all different and didn't seem to be the same species. Was there such a thing for these creatures? One had long, floppy ears, long whiskers, and a lean body covered in what looked like slime. Another had short horns, four narrow yellow eyes, and a mouth that could eat me whole. A third one had a huge, bald head and long fangs curling over its upper lip. And the last one had an almost round body with what looked like fins on his back, and membranes under its arm that seemed like wings.

Holy shit, I had hit my head harder than I thought and was now dreaming about this craziness. That was the only explanation for all of this.

I focused and called my magic ... and only a flicker answered me. The pain in my head increased and my breathing grew heavy. I had exhausted most of my magic before, and I needed rest to recharge it, but I didn't have many options here! I tried again, gently coaxing my magic to come to me, to be the avalanche I needed now. I promised it that later I would really, really rest.

But nothing happened. When I seemed to reach it, the pain in my head only intensified to the point of making me dizzy.

No, this couldn't be it. I would keep trying. However, the creatures exchanged some sounds I couldn't make out—was this their language?—and I lost my train of thought.

They slowed down a little and then the two creatures in front of the procession disappeared. I jerked against the creature holding me, and it only tightened its grip around me.

The creature to my right jumped forward a foot—and then was swallowed by the ground. What?

Then I saw it. A dozen huge holes in the ground. Before I could process it, the creature carrying me jumped into one. My stomach flipped and I yelped.

The creature landed hard in what looked like a huge, underground tunnel. It followed the other creatures to an archway and into a large cave—a room deep below the earth.

Right in the center, a creature, uglier and a lot larger than the others, sat in what looked like a chair made of ... oh my God, my stomach revolved—skin! It looked like human skin.

Panic rushed through me. Even though I trembled from head to toe, I pushed the panic back and tried assessing the situation. This bigger creature seemed to be the leader, the boss.

The creature carrying me stopped a few yards from the boss and tossed me at its feet. I landed hard on my side and almost hit my head again.

The creatures talked again in their rumbly, clicky language.

Then the boss surprised me. "Hello, little witch," it said, its voice deep and with a heavy accent. I gaped at it, at a loss for words. A rumble that sounded like a cough mixed with snorts came from the creature and it took me a moment to realize it was laughing. "You surprised? Just like others."

That piqued my interest and pushed through the other three hundred questions that had popped in my mind before. I rolled to my side and sat up, the ropes tugging at my skin. "Others?"

"We see others in our lands," it said. "Some, we scare away. Some, we capture. Some ... we eat." The boss laughed again, and this time the other creatures joined in.

I glanced around, horrified by this place, this situation. I was in a lair deep in the earth, facing a monster, and surrounded by dozens of crazed beasts who all seemed eager to eat me alive.

How was I going to get out of this one?

A new wave of fear chilled my spine and I looked for my magic again. It sparked, but I knew I wouldn't be able to do more than break my ropes and throw a bolt or two before I collapsed of either pain or exhaustion. Or both.

There was no way for me to safely get out of here.

The boss showed me its large teeth in what I thought was a freaky smile. "Time to get ready."

I swallowed my fear. "Ready? For?"

It licked its lips with its forked tongue. "Dinner."

23

KILLIAN

I WALKED INTO VULZAL'S LAIR AS IF I WAS A GUEST. NO monster stopped me, but they all watched me. Some followed me, some snarled at me, some jumped in front of me and snapped their jaws as if that would scare me away.

I had already caught Lavinia's scent on the outside and it was stronger in here. Nothing, not even if the monsters in here attacked me, would stop me from getting to her.

I emerged into the central, bigger room in the underground lair, and just as I expected, Lavinia was before Vulzal, her hands and feet bound, and her face pale while Vulzal told her, in a subtle way, that she was going to be his dinner.

Over my dead body.

I cleared my throat.

Vulzal turned to me, and Lavinia gasped.

"Killian."

I didn't look at her. Instead, I held Vulzal's unflinching gaze.

"Ah, the vampire," Vulzal said. The leader leaned back

into his skin-covered chair. I had seen it a couple of times before, but it always made me sick. "It has been a long time."

"Hand her to me," I said, my voice dead serious.

The monster let out his awkward laughter. "I hungry," he said in his broken English.

When I first met him, I was shocked he knew English at all, but he revealed he had captured a supernatural before and had forced him to teach him our language ... before eating him.

"And she smell delicious."

He licked his lips and I almost jumped at him right then. That big, nasty mouth wouldn't come anywhere close to Lavinia.

"Let her go, and I'll give you a cup of my blood," I offered. One of my worst scars had been from when Vulzal slashed my back with his nail and had taken it to his mouth. After that, the monster hadn't stopped telling me how much he craved my blood. Vulzal kept saying it would cut me in large chunks and dip my meat in my blood.

"What? Killian, no," Lavinia said. She had pushed to her knees, but I was still avoiding her gaze.

Vulzal's face scrunched in what looked like a scowl. "You lie. You lie before."

So did Vulzal. Before, when he had first caught me and wanted to eat me, I offered to catch others like me and work for him if he let me live. At the time, I'd had no idea what I was talking about. I had never seen anyone like me there, but I had been ready to throw any lies so he wouldn't kill me. Dumb as most monsters, Vulzal agreed.

And then I ran without caring for my promise.

But in this land, there was nowhere to run. I roamed for ... I didn't know, days? Weeks? Months? Trying to find a way to leave this place, or put more distance between Vulzal and me, but the land was fluid. I always ended up near the lair again.

Vulzal had me caught again.

We'd played this game far too often. By now, Vulzal knew he couldn't kill me easily, but the opposite was also true.

"I'm not lying now," I said.

Vulzal made a groaning sound. "Just one cup?"

"Two. That's the most I can offer."

"Killian, you can't!" Lavinia shouted.

Vulzal shook his head. "Five cups."

I scoffed. If I let him have five cups, I wouldn't die, but I would be too tired to take Lavinia and me safely out of here. Because I didn't trust Vulzal to follow through on his promise. The moment he released Lavinia, he would attack, I was sure of that.

"A little greedy, old man?" I teased.

"Always," Vulzal answered, without missing a beat.

"Bring the cups," I said.

"Killian!" Lavinia called me. I finally glanced at her. Her eyes were as big as basketballs. "What the hell are you doing?"

"Be ready," I whispered.

She stared at me as if I was crazy.

Vulzal spoke to another monster in their own language. The monster walked away to fetch the cups.

I acted.

In my super speed, I ran to Lavinia, ripped off the ropes around her arms and legs, and picked her up in my arms.

The monsters roared.

I kept running toward the exit. "If you can, do something," I told Lavinia.

Lavinia reached around my shoulders and sent a wave of magic toward the monsters, pushing them back. Then she collapsed against me. "Too ... weak ..." she muttered, her eyes fluttering.

Shit. "No, hang in there. We're almost out of here."

A rumble shook the walls of the tunnels, and the passage just a few feet from us collapsed. I skidded to a stop before we both hit the new wall of dirt in front of us. I turned and saw Vulzal stalking toward us. I glanced around, but there was no other exit, no other tunnel forking in this corner.

"Stupid vampire," Vulzal said as he got closer.

I lowered Lavinia's legs. "Can you stand?"

She nodded, but when I started pulling my arms back, she slipped to the ground. I held on to her. Shit, it was worse than I thought. I leaned her back against the tunnel's wall behind me. "Hang on."

I rolled my shoulders and faced Vulzal. The leader covered the entire tunnel, but I knew there were plenty more monsters behind him. This wouldn't be pretty.

Vulzal came at me like a bull. I met the monster headfirst and held him back with all of my strength. If I let it go, Vulzal would crush me and Lavinia. I threw my weight to the left, successfully pulling the monster with me. He reached with his big hands and sharp nails toward me. I swung under his arms and rotated to his back. The monster turned to me.

Hands grabbed me from behind. More monsters.

"No," Lavinia whispered. She threw her hand out and a wave of magic brushed gently against me, but hit the monsters holding me like a rock. They flew back, and a blue shield covered the tunnel, blocking the monsters out. Now it was just Vulzal, Lavinia, and me in this small space.

Enraged, Vulzal swiped a hand at me. I dodged the attack.

But that was just a distraction. With his other hand, he grabbed Lavinia. Vulzal's claws sank into her chest.

Lavinia groaned and fell back like a rag doll, bright red blooming on her clothes.

"No!" I shouted.

My fangs elongated, my face transformed, and a sea of red covered my vision. I jumped at Vulzal. I punched through his chest and sank my entire arm in his body. I grabbed what I thought was his huge heart and squeezed it until it popped like a grape.

Vulzal's body went limp and fell forward. I jumped from him before being squashed. Taking off my shirt and cleaning my arm with it, I ran to Lavinia. I tossed my shirt aside and crouched beside her.

"Lavinia," I called her, cradling her in my arms. Shit, there was so much red. So much red! "My love, talk to me."

Her eyes fluttered open, but they didn't fix on anything. "Killian," she whispered. A sob broke through her lips. "I'm sorry."

My chest tightened. Another red cloak covered my entire soul. No, no, no, this couldn't be it. But as I took a good look at her wounds, I knew this was it. Vulzal had pierced her lungs and her stomach, and scratched her heart.

She gasped for air.

"Please hang on." I gathered her in my arms, and turned to the only exit—where the shield still held and a hundred monsters waited for me, roaring with their own pain.

We would never make it out of here. Not in time to save her.

I held her tight. "Please, hang on," I repeated.

"It's okay," she whispered. She reached up and brushed her fingers against my cheek.

Then her arm dropped like a stone. Her breathing and her heart stopped.

"NO!" I roared.

My insides twisted, my mind went blank, and my vision was pure red. This couldn't be it. This couldn't be happening. There was no way I had found my mate and had already lost her.

There had to be another way.

There was ...

I stared at Lavinia's pale face.

Shit, I hoped she would forgive me.

I sank my fangs into her throat and drank. I drank enough to make this work. Then I bit my wrist, opening two small punctures and letting my blood out. I pressed my wrist to her mouth, angling it so the blood dripped into her mouth and slid down her throat.

"Come on, come on, come on," I muttered under my breath. I had never turned anyone before, but I had seen it done several times. I knew what I had to do.

It had to work.

I counted the seconds like they were decades, until finally her breathing and heartbeat came back, and her mouth closed around my wrist. She reached up and grasped my arm, pulling it closer.

I sighed in relief.

"That's enough," I told her, prying her from my arm. "That's enough."

Lavinia blinked, her eyes wild, her movements jerky. She glanced side to side and recoiled from me. "What happened?" She looked at her quavering hands. "Oh my God, what's happening to me?" She pressed her hands to her stomach. "I feel sick. No, I feel dead."

"Lavinia ..."

She looked down at herself, at all the blood on her clothes, on the ground, at Vulzal's body behind me.

She shook her head. "What did you do?"

I raised my open palms up. "I know you're in shock, but listen to me. It was the only way." The monsters slammed into the shield, and it trembled and flickered. It wouldn't hold for long. "Listen, we can argue about this later, but right now, we need to get out of here." Thankfully, her body was reacting well to the change. I shot up and offered my hand to her. "I know you're probably feeling disoriented, your senses too raw, your hunger painful, and much more. But try to focus on being fast and getting out of this place alive? We'll figure out the rest later, okay?"

She stared at my hand. The shield flickered again. Finally, she slipped her hand in mine and stood with me. "Okay."

THE SHIELD BROKE a few seconds later, and I took the lead by running as fast as I could through the tunnels, weaving past the monsters intent on killing us. I paid attention, but from the sound of it, Lavinia was having no problem keeping up. I ran past the hole in the ground and surged outside. I turned and waited for Lavinia.

Only a handful of seconds later, she appeared by my side. And promptly sat on the hard ground, her breathing shallow and her hand over her stomach.

I crouched beside. "What is it?"

She groaned.

A monster came up from the hole and advanced on us. More followed. Lavinia extended her hand and a blue ball shot from her open palm. It expanded and stretched, turning into a blanket that covered the holes, trapping the monsters in.

Except one.

It was a small monster, not much larger than I was, and not too fast on its hoofed feet. I met it headfirst, ducked under the slow swipe of its heavy arm, and quickly reached up and broke its neck.

Its body crumpled to the ground with a muffled thud.

Monster forgotten, I stared at Lavinia. She seemed paler than usual, the black lines around her eyes appearing and fading away every few seconds, and she braced her stomach —it was normal. Each person reacted a little different after turning. A small percentage of newer vampires experienced what we called blood rage. The hunger and the need for blood took over right away and they lost all other senses and consciousness. They became animals. It was hard to bring back a vampire from that. Most were hunted and killed.

The majority, though, felt sick and in excruciating pain for a few days. Their hunger was acute, but with constant feeding and guidance, those vampires ended up all right.

A small percentage took it well and had minor changes— which thankfully was what I was seeing with Lavinia. I had taken a gamble when I turned her in the middle of a fight, but I'd had no other choice. I wouldn't let her die on my watch. For new vampires, their hair grew longer, their skin smoothed a little, their eyes became shinier and their lashes longer, stuff like that—and some body pains, some nausea, and sensitivity from the heightened senses. Those passed in a couple of days, or a week at most.

But the most surprising was the fact that she still could access her magic. Usually, when a supernatural turned, she or he lost any sign of their previous species. Only a rare handful retained it.

However, Lavinia had created a mesh of magic to trap the monsters as if it was nothing, while she was in pain and nauseated. A few moments ago, her magic wasn't even responding to her anymore, which reinforced what I knew about her all along: Lavinia was special. At least to me.

Slowly, I approached her. "How are you feeling?"

She wrinkled her nose. "Like I ate some really bad sushi."

At least her sense of humor was intact. "That is your body changing, adapting, and taking my blood in your system. It'll pass." She stared at me with her big, hazel eyes. A fist closed around my heart. Damn, I had almost lost her. "Lavinia, you might be mad with me right now, but you have to understand —you died. You just ... died. I couldn't take it. I did the only thing I could do."

Tears brimmed in her eyes. "I know," she whispered. "I'm still trying to wrap my head around what happened, and to control this crazy hunger and this shitty pain, but ... I know." She offered me a tight smile. "I would have done the same."

Shit, that was good to hear. I reached for her, afraid of being too pushy while she was still struggling with the change, but she met me halfway. She threw herself in my arms. I held her tight, buried my face on her neck and hair, and inhaled deeply. Her scent had changed slightly, but it was even more alluring than before.

Emotion filled my chest. "I love you so much."

"I love you too," she whispered. Lavinia pulled back a little, looked me in the eyes, then pressed her lips to mine. Holy shit ... I accepted that kiss and took control, deepening it. She tasted of my blood and it was such a turn on.

She moved her hips ever so slightly, but enough to elicit a groan from my throat. Damn, this woman drove me nuts.

Bright lightning followed by a clap of thunder cut through the dark skies, and Lavinia startled. She pressed her hands over her ears.

I placed my hands over hers. "Yeah, it'll feel uncomfortable at first, but I promise you, you'll get used to it."

Slowly, she lowered her hands. "So ... I'm now a vampire too." I nodded. "And a witch."

"And still technically half-demon hunter."

"Well, that side of myself never really manifested."

"True, but your magic seemed stronger a moment ago, maybe the demon hunter side will come out more now."

She frowned. "Is it possible? To be more than one thing?"

"It's rare to turn into a vampire and still hold to the affinities of your previous species," I told her truthfully. "But we can talk about that with Drake, Thea, and Almae later. I bet one of them will know about this." I sighed. "For now, we should really get some distance from the tunnels and figure out how to get back."

"First, let me say thank you. For coming after me."

I scoffed. "As if there was any other choice."

She smiled. I lost the battle of my self-control and kissed her again, even though we really should get moving. Really, even if I was dying to make love to her again, it wouldn't be in this shitty land, on this hard ground, while she was still struggling with the change and monsters could attack.

With great difficulty, I held on to her and stood up, bringing her along with me. I placed a quick peck on her lips, entwined her fingers in mine, and tugged her closer. "Let's get out of here."

24

___

LAVINIA

Never in a million years would I have thought I would turn into a vampire. Ever since Killian turned me, everything felt intense, loud, bright, and my stomach had stopped hurting.

I could hear our footsteps crunching the hard ground underneath our feet, the brush of our clothes as we walked, the soft and warm wind blowing against us. I could feel how hot it was, how this land was dry and dead.

I also felt the hunger deep in my core. Whenever it struck me, I felt my fangs extending and the skin around my eyes tightening as the black lines appeared. I had tasted Killian's blood—it was what brought me back to life—and as much as it appealed to me right now, I knew that warm blood from a deer would be the most delicious thing I had ever tasted.

Before, the thought of being a vampire and drinking blood made me sick, but now ... now it was all I could think about, all I wanted. When Killian killed that last creature, I thought about latching myself to it and drinking its blood! Whether it would taste good, that was another subject.

In silence and holding hands, Killian and I walked away from the creatures' lair without any real direction. Not that there were any landmarks or way of telling where we were going.

Whenever we heard a creature approaching, we ran the other way.

And that made me think of Killian alone here for twenty years.

"I'm sorry," I whispered.

He glanced at me. "For?"

"For bringing you back here. I know you hate this place."

He let out a long sigh. "I do hate it, but I told you, Lavinia, I would jump headfirst into hell if you were there."

That warmed my heart. My dead heart? I put a hand over my heart to feel it. I gasped. "It's still beating."

Killian nodded. "It's normal. For most people, the heart doesn't just stop. It slows down gradually. In a day or two, it'll stop completely."

It was so odd to think my heart would stop. Yeah, there were things I still needed time to process, to understand, to come to terms with. But Killian was right. Now wasn't the time. We had to focus on getting out of here first.

But how?

Suddenly, we heard swift footsteps approaching and a rapid heartbeat. Killian and I tensed and prepared to run away, but then the breeze blew and brought in her scent.

"Twyla," I whispered, amazed.

"Yes," Killian said. He narrowed his eyes at me.

At first, I didn't get why he looked at me that way, but once Twyla reached us, I knew. The beat of her heart grew louder in my ears, as did the rush of the blood in her veins. Her warm, warm blood. It sang to me, almost as loud as the boxes' magic had done.

I stared at her, entranced.

Killian cleared his throat.

And I snapped out of it. I let go of his hand and took several steps back.

Twyla didn't slow down. She ran at me at top speed.

Killian stepped in her way and pushed her back.

"Don't touch me!" she shouted. "She put me in here again. I'll kick her ass."

Hands raised, Killian said, "Not right now. She's a new vampire and you shouldn't get too close."

Twyla stumbled two steps back, her eyes wide. "What?'

"Long story," Killian muttered. "She's back to herself. Sort of. Her bloodlust is still a new thing. Just ... keep your distance for now." Twyla nodded, her gaze on me. "Don't worry. If anything happens, I'll intervene."

"If you say so," she muttered.

Damn, this was hard. I could hear her freaking blood inside her veins! I took five steps back and looked up, at the lightning cutting through the dark skies, and focused on the sound of the thunder shaking the earth.

"Have you found anyone else?" Killian asked.

"No," Twyla answered. "I've never met anyone else before. I don't know how we were lucky to meet now."

"We just ..." Killian let out a long breath. "We should find a place to hide and wait. When Almae opens the boxes, we'll come out, like before."

"*If* Almae opens the boxes," Twyla said.

"Think positive." Killian walked to me and took my hand

in his. We started walking, a good twenty feet between Twyla and us.

He started telling her all that had happened since I put her back in the box—which I felt really bad for—but I tuned them out and focused on the lightning and thunder. It was the only way to take Twyla's blood from my mind.

We walked through this dark world for hours, or was it days? At some point, we stopped to rest—Twyla far from me. We encountered creatures twice, and both times, I stayed far away, using my magic to fight them. I was afraid that if I got too close, if I engaged in a more physical fight, I would lose control and attack Twyla.

Then we stopped and rested again.

The hunger was getting the best of me, and while I sat down and leaned on Killian's shoulder, dreams of drinking from Twyla filled my mind. Holy shit, if this continued, I would have to ask her to leave.

Otherwise, I would kill her.

I must had fallen asleep, because the next thing I knew, Killian was shaking me awake.

"Lavinia, wake up," he said, pulling on my hands. My eyes fluttered open. I was already standing, thanks to him, and stilled at the sight in front of me.

Almae stood a handful of feet from us, her hands outstretched. "Come on. Time to get out of here."

It was the same as Twyla. Her warmth, her scent, her blood ... Dear lord. I started retreating, but Killian locked his hand with mine and took Almae's. Twyla slipped her hand into Almae's too.

Smoke swirled around us, making the world spin for a minute.

Then it slowly faded.

My senses were hammered—so many people around us, bright lights overhead, the sound of the fire crackling in the fireplace, of voices talking together, the heartbeat of several people, their scent, and oh God, so much blood inside their veins.

I pressed a hand over my ears and Killian embraced me, purposefully wrapping his arms around my head. "Lavinia is a vampire," he said, his tone loud and clear. The room went *almost* silent. "She needs a moment to gather herself." He picked me up and ran away.

I felt the rush of cold air against my body when we stepped outside. After a few seconds, Killian set me down on a rocking chair and crouched down in front of me. Not trusting myself, I glanced around.

We were on a porch of a ... I squinted, reading the hanging wooden sign from the post outside the porch—a bed and breakfast. The sun was setting behind a large, wooded area, but in the distance I could see roofs, chimneys, and smoke.

"Where are we?" I asked in a low voice.

"I'm not sure," he said. His eyes fixed on mine. "Lavinia, you haven't really fed since you turned. We probably should do that before anything else."

I swallowed hard. Feed. Hunting. Drinking blood from animals. It was both exciting and disgusting. But I knew Killian was right. Perhaps if I fed, if I became completely full on blood, I would be able to get closer to the others without dreaming about attacking them. And then I would be able to focus and learn how to control my senses, especially how to drown out the sounds so they wouldn't drive me crazy.

I nodded.

Killian took my hand in his, and together, we ran into the woods behind the B&B.

THE HUNT HAD BEEN EXHILARATING and disgusting at the same time. Killian helped track deer. He caught two of them for us and showed me where to bite.

The blood had been warm and delicious, and I ended up draining the entire deer in a matter of seconds.

But I definitely felt better after. More in control.

As Killian and I made our way back to the B&B, I took that time to work on my senses. I heard the crunch and rustling of leaves, the sounds of small crickets, even the breeze blowing in the distance. It had gotten darker while we were out but I still could see almost everything, and a lot farther and sharper than before.

It was amazing.

"How are you feeling?" Killian asked.

"Better."

"Good." He squeezed my hand. "I was afraid you would resent me for turning you into a vampire."

"I already told you, I would have done the same."

"I know, but this is all brand new. You might still change your mind."

"Do you plan on breaking up with me?"

Killian stared at me with a deep, fierce frown. "Never."

"Then I won't change my mind." He tugged me closer and placed a kiss on the top of my head. I let out a sigh. "But like you said, it's still all brand new. I'm trying to get used to it."

"You just turned. Maybe a couple of hours ago? It's hard to keep track of time while in that realm. Anyway, it takes weeks to get used to everything, every little change, if not months. All things considered, you're doing amazingly."

I would have blushed if my body still worked that way. It was good to hear that because I felt like I was failing.

We approached the B&B and Drake was on the porch, his arms crossed, his shoulder leaning against a wooden pillar, waiting for us. He looked impeccable with black slacks and a black shirt. Any human would have looked at him and said he was a powerful billionaire. The man exuded power and finesse.

"We need to talk," he said.

Killian and I stopped a few feet from the porch. Killian nodded. "We do."

Drake went straight to the point. "What happened when you were gone?"

After a long exhale, Killian told him about killing Eldon, finding me in Vulzal's lair, our tentative escape, and my death. I shuddered, remembering it.

Then he told Drake about miraculously finding Twyla and Almae showing up to get us out of there.

Drake looked at me. "Have you fed? How are you feeling?"

"I'm ... a little overwhelmed, but now that I've fed, I'm feeling a little better." I shifted my weight. "I think I can control myself now, but I would rather still be very careful."

"It's unusual for vampires to be this controlled. Usually, they don't think straight and aren't so well mannered. All they want is blood, and they do almost anything for it. It's a long and hard process to control oneself." Drake narrowed his eyes. "But here you are, unlike anything I've seen in my five hundred years. Just a warning: Don't hold it against our friends if they are wary of you, at least in the beginning."

I nodded.

"What about here?" Killian asked. "Where are we?"

"After you two disappeared with Eldon, and Dommik left with a couple of his vampires, the fighting died down. The remaining warlocks and vampires either ran or surrendered ... and the ones who ran were hunted and killed." Drake sighed. "We couldn't let Dommik have the boxes, so we occupied this bed and breakfast near his coven. We compelled the humans to stay away from us and forget if they see anything strange. As for Almae, she met us here so she could open the box and rescue you."

"Wait, how long were we in the box?" I asked.

It took Drake a couple of seconds to say, "A little over two days."

Oh, wow. We had been in the box for two days? I had felt maybe like half a day? But it certainly hadn't felt that long at all.

Behind Drake, the door opened and Almae and Thea walked out. I retreated another step, afraid of my reaction to them.

"It's okay," Thea said with a smile. She halted beside Drake. "You won't hurt us, and even if you try, we will stop you before you do. Don't worry."

Almae didn't stop beside them. She kept walking toward me. I took another two steps back. "Thea speaks the truth, my dear. You won't hurt us. Believe that."

I planted my foot on the ground, my senses picking up her warmth, her heartbeat, the blood in her veins. Shit. "I want to believe that, but I would rather be careful for now."

Almae halted three feet from me. "I can help you." She reached for my hand. "With magic."

I frowned but didn't resist it. She enveloped my hands in

hers and her magic surrounded me. Mine joined instantly, and together, they gave me a sense of calm and control. The hunger, the senses, it was all pushed back and became a dull pulse at the back of my head. I didn't think it would get better than this, but it was already a miracle.

I gasped, as if I could finally breathe again. "This is amazing. Thank you."

She smiled at me and pulled me into a tight hug. "Oh, my dear, anything for you."

The front door opened again and two more people stepped out of the B&B. Almae pulled back and gestured for them to get closer. "Lavinia, this is my son, Keeran, and his mate, Luana." She cupped her mouth. "She's the alpha of the Starlight wolves."

Wow ... I stared at my cousin and his beautiful mate. So he was the new Warlock Lord after Soren, but he now had another name. From the little I had heard, he had changed the course of the warlock coven—the ones who remained with him, at least—and she was a freaking alpha? I had no idea what a Starlight wolf was, but it sounded impressive.

"Hi," I said tentatively.

Keeran showed me a brief smile before hugging me. Then it was Luana's turn. I felt dazed and weird. They were strangers, but they were also family. The only thing I truly knew was that they all liked to hug. And honestly, after a lifetime of isolation and trying to keep my distance from everyone, it was nice to have close friends and family.

I hugged them back.

"It's so great to finally meet you," Keeran said.

"We're family now," Luana said. "If you need anything, let us know."

I frowned. Besides destroying the boxes and freeing the

supernaturals inside ... my eyes widened. "Eldon had several supernaturals in the basement. He was going to put them in the empty boxes." With my help. "What happened to them?"

"We freed them," Drake said. "Two of them left, but a friend of ours stayed."

I frowned. "Who?"

"Ariella, the angel."

I nodded. I remembered when Eldon and the others showed her to me, how they talked about hurting her, torturing her, and I didn't even care. That made me sick to my stomach. "Is she okay? Is she hurt?"

Thea shook her head. "No, she's fine. She said they talked big, but didn't do much."

"Good." Then I remembered someone else. "What about Twyla? Is she here?"

"She is," Thea said. "She was tired, though, so Shane took her to a bedroom to rest."

Twyla and I had talked a bit about what happened, but it wasn't enough. Now that I felt more like myself—my new, hyper-sensitive and aware self—I wanted to ask for her forgiveness again.

"One of the boxes the warlocks had was occupied," I told them. "A female werewolf. They left her in there."

"Many of the boxes that Delia hid still have supernaturals in them," Almae said. "We plan on rescuing them all after this mess is done."

I nodded, liking this plan.

"All right, I think we straightened out most of the wrinkles," Drake said. "Go feed or rest or eat or whatever. Be ready, because in less than thirty minutes, we're attacking the Dark Devils."

He took Thea's hand and went inside the B&B. Almae

patted my shoulder and followed them, along with Keeran and Luana.

Then it was Killian and me outside.

He turned to me and slid his hands around my waist, pulling me to him. "Are you okay to fight? It's okay if you aren't. You can stay here and we'll come back soon."

I shook my head and wrapped my arms around his neck. "No, I want to go. Whatever Almae did to me, it's working. I feel much more in control now."

"Good." He rested his forehead on mine. "This will be your first official fight as a vampire."

"I know." I groaned. "I don't know what I should rely on. The vampire part or my magic."

"I would say your magic since you're more used to it. But if things get ugly and you can't cast a spell, let your fangs out and go for the throat."

I wrinkled my nose. "Great visual."

"Glad to help." The corners of his lips curled up, and I chuckled. He grew serious again. "I know this is selfish, but I'm glad you're a vampire now."

"Oh yeah?"

He nodded, his forehead rubbing on mine. "As a witch, you would live a lot longer than humans, but you wouldn't be immortal. One day in the distant future, you would leave me. Now you won't."

My heart skipped a beat at his words. If he wanted to spend the rest of his immortality with me, then it was a fact: He genuinely loved me.

I rose on my tiptoes and pressed my lips to his. A groan rumbled from his chest as he melded his mouth with mine and deepened the kiss. His hands skimmed under my sweater and teased my bare skin. A shiver like none I had before rocked my body. Holy shit ... I gasped, amazed about how heightened all of my senses were, even touch. If kissing him, if touching him was like this, damn, I couldn't wait until he was inside me again.

"Hey, lovebirds."

Killian broke the kiss and snarled at Shane, who stood on the porch.

"Don't kill the messenger." He raised his hands in a peace sign. "Drake is calling. We'll be leaving soon."

He didn't wait for a response and went back in the B&B. Killian kissed me once more, fast, hard, and deep, leaving me breathless, and then pulled away. His eyes were dark and his body seemed to be humming with pent-up energy.

I knew the feeling.

Killian inhaled deeply and took my hand in his. "Ready?"

I wasn't, not really. "Yes."

25

KILLIAN

WE FORMED QUITE THE TEAM—DRAKE, THEA, KEERAN, Luana, Shane, Twyla, Elisa, Zadkiel, Dorian, Aston, Gray, Cain, Patrick, Ariella, Lavinia, and me. Almae had come too, despite Keeran's protests. We approached the Dark Devils' lair in silence.

I didn't know this place. When I had last seen them, they lived in a mansion in downtown Coquitlam. It hadn't been great when you wanted to keep a secret of who you really were.

Now, they lived at a contemporary mansion, at the bottom of a hill, just outside of Coquitlam. Behind the mansion, there were plenty of smaller houses, probably to house their vampires—the ones we had killed most of during the last battle.

We didn't know how many of them were left, so we decided to be careful. We stayed beyond the trees around the property and listened and watched for any sign of the vampires. We didn't want them to hear us, so we probably couldn't hear them either.

Thea and Elisa cast spells that enhanced Drake's hearing and vision even more.

"I hear them inside," he said in a low voice. He lifted a hand and we tensed in anticipation. He dropped the hand.

Go.

I glanced at Lavinia by my side, held her hand, and both of us zoomed past the trees, across the terrain, toward the house along with all the others. Like an avalanche, the sixteen of us invaded the mansion and stopped, setting our stances ready for a fight.

I glanced around. There was no one here. No sound, no voices, no life. What the …?

Drake exited the house and we followed him, but we couldn't get far. A dark circle marked a wide perimeter around the house, and beyond the circle were Dommik, some of his vampires, Tack, a handful of his warlocks … and Patrick.

I advanced on him, ready to rip out his throat, but the moment I reached the circle's line, I was pushed back by magic.

"You bastard!" I shouted.

Drake stood beside me, just as pissed as I was. "What is going on? Patrick, explain yourself!"

A smile stretched across Patrick's face. "Finally, I'll get rid of you," he said to me. "And bonus points for getting rid of all of you." He pointedly looked at all the princes and Drake.

"You were one of us," Drake said, his voice loaded.

"Honestly, I never felt like it," Patrick said. "It took me decades to get a chance to prove myself, but then what happened? I had to compete with this moron." He gestured to me. "And I was losing. Lord Reynard sent you on a mission to talk to Dommik, and I knew that if you succeeded in that, I was done for. It would take me another hundred years to have a chance to become a prince again. I couldn't stand it. I couldn't stand you. So when I found out Soren needed a vampire for his spell, I set it up with him. I facilitated your kidnapping. I became a prince." His smile shone bright for another two seconds, then it faded. "Then you came back and you brought a witch bitch with you."

"You—" I advanced again, intent on crossing the circle's magic somehow, but Drake closed his hand around my arm and kept me back.

"I took her from DuMoir Castle and handed her to Tack and the others," Patrick continued. "Later, I told Eldon that Lavinia had broken through the darkness and was pretending to be under their control." A foot behind me, Lavinia gasped in shock. "There were a few detours, but we finally got here. To the end."

I clenched my fists. "Yes, it'll be the end. Your end, because I'll kill you, you bastard!"

Patrick laughed. "I would like to see you try."

Tack closed his eyes and lifted his hands. The circle hummed as fire rose from the perimeter and advanced toward us. Behind us, someone screamed.

"It's magical fire," Drake said. "Don't get near it. It can kill us."

We retreated a few steps. "I don't think we have much choice here."

Lavinia stayed close to me, her hands on my back. "There must be something we can do."

"There is," Thea said, stepping closer. "At least, I hope so." Matching Tack's stance, Thea closed her eyes and moved her hands out.

Almae stepped to Thea's side, along with Keeran and

Elisa. The four of them joined their magic and pushed back against the fire. Lavinia narrowed her eyes and turned alongside them, adding her magic to the mix.

Four powerful witches and a powerful warlock against Tack and his measly lackeys. He had the advantage here, because of the circle's added power, but he had underestimated our side.

The fire retreated. Dommik and Patrick yelled for Tack and his handful of warlocks to work harder to kill us.

For a moment, the fire was at a standstill. It didn't advance and it didn't retreat.

Until our witches and warlock moved in unison, as if they were connected on an astral level. They twisted their hands in the same way, retreated their hands in the same way, and threw them out, palms forward, in the same way.

The fire rolled out of the circle in a huge wave, advancing on our enemies. They shouted and ran away. But it wasn't done. The witches and Keeran continued working. They weaved their hands, controlling the fire that now spread wide like a glowing snake and encircled our enemies.

"Our circle is broken," Thea said.

That was all we needed to hear. I ran toward Patrick. Drake went for Dommik. Keeran struck Tack. The other vampires and warlocks were picked up by the rest of our group.

Patrick faced me, his fangs out. "You're scum. The lowest of the low. You can't kill me."

"You know I like to prove you wrong." I lunged at him, my fangs bared.

Patrick moved aside when I came for him, but I expected that. When he fell to the right, I turned too and barreled into him, my hands going for his throat. Patrick's eyes widened as he wasn't expecting that move, and he leaned back. My fingers grazed his neck before he swiped his arm down and pushed my hands back.

He turned for a kick, but I put an arm out, blocking it, and immediately struck again, this time with a kick of my own. It hit his side and made him stagger back two steps, but Patrick was also a vampire—he was fast and agile and capable. And I suspected that in the twenty years I had been gone, he had improved, while I had survived in that dark land.

We exchanged a series of fast, hard strikes, trying to hit each other and gain the advantage. All the while, I paid little attention to our surroundings—to how Keeran and Tack, and Drake and Dommik were in a similar match, fighting against supernaturals almost as strong as they were. Meanwhile, Lavinia, Thea, Almae, and Elisa stayed back, sending bolts of magic toward the vampires or warlocks who tried running away, or the ones who went for them. Our team attacked the rest of them head on.

A scream caught my attention and I turned toward it. Still inside the circle, Lavinia was on the ground, and a vampire jumped over her. My muscles locked for a second and my brain decided to go to her, but before I could move, she transformed. The black veins appeared around her eyes, and her fangs extended. She snarled. Blue snakes wound around her arms and wrapped around the vampire's legs, holding him in place. Then she went for his throat.

She killed him in matter of seconds.

Pride and worry filled me.

A second later, I landed on the hard ground, Patrick on top of me. He bared his fangs and went for my neck. Shit. He had taken advantage of my distraction to get the better of me. His fangs snapped less than an inch from my skin and I used all of my strength to push him away. But he was stronger than me. More experienced.

My arms struggled with the effort. I tried using my legs to push him away, jerk my body to destabilize him, but nothing seem to work. My arms started giving out.

Oh shit.

"Die, you prick," he said, his fangs shining. He came for my throat.

A blue snake wrapped around his arms and his torso. Involuntarily, Patrick stood up while the snake wound around his legs too.

Standing a couple of feet to the side, Lavinia looked at me. "I would love to kill him myself, but I won't take that honor from you." She withdrew the blue magical snake.

I zoomed from the ground to Patrick, who had been distracted by the magic and Lavinia. I closed my mouth on his throat and went for the jugular. I ripped out half of his neck and stepped back, letting his body fall to the ground.

"Are you okay?" I asked Lavinia.

She nodded, her fangs and the black veins gone.

I glanced around. The fighting seemed to be dying out as fewer vampires and warlocks fought against our group. Dommik lay motionless at Drake's feet. Keeran stood beside Drake.

"Where's Tack?" I asked.

"Keeran smoked him," she said. "Literally."

Frowning, I entwined my hand with Lavinia's and approached Drake and Keeran. Thea, Almae, and Luana also walked toward us. The rest of our group rounded up the last of our enemies in the circle.

Cain dragged a vampire toward us. The vampire held a black duffel bag. "Give it to him."

Shaking, the vampire dropped the bag at Drake's feet. Wary, Drake opened the bag. "The boxes." He picked up the bag and slung it across his shoulders.

"What do I do with him?" Cain asked.

Drake considered it for a second. "Let him go." He looked out at the supernaturals in the circle. "Let them all go."

Cain went back to the circle and passed the message along.

I watched, my frown deepening. "Why?"

"Because the leaders are dead," Drake said, his tone somber. "Without a leader to guide them, most of these vampires and warlocks won't do anything. Besides, I want DuMoir Castle to be remembered as a strong and fearless coven, but also merciful. We aren't evil. We don't kill because we can."

I nodded, understanding what he meant. I stared at him and for the first time, I actually felt something. Before, I had been so passionate about Lord Reynard being our leader, I hadn't opened up to the idea of Drake being in his place. With the occurrences of the last couple of weeks, I had accepted it. But now I saw that Drake could be an even better leader for DuMoir Castle.

I squeezed Lavinia's hand. With Drake at the helm, and her by my side, I dared to get a little excited about the future.

26

LAVINIA

ONCE WE WERE BACK AND SAFE AT DUMOIR CASTLE, ALMAE, Keeran, and I went to the back garden where we recreated the large white circle with the fifteen points. Killian, Luana, Drake, and Thea followed us, but kept their distance.

The three of us placed the seven boxes in their spots on the circle and stepped out. Almae picked up a dagger from her skirt and pressed the tip of her finger to the blade. A drop of blood bloomed against her skin. She handed the dagger to Keeran and he did the same. He passed the dagger to me. I sucked in a sharp breath before pushing the blade into my skin. It was only a quick prick, but I hissed anyway.

I returned the dagger to Almae and she pocketed it again. She extended her arm in front of her and let the blood drip into the circle. Keeran and I did the same.

The drops of blood sizzled upon contact with the ground in the circle, and suddenly, the circle began to hum. The hum intensified and I could feel it inside me, vibrating in my chest, in my veins. It was connected to me, to my blood, to my magic.

Almae closed her eyes, chanting in a low voice in a language I didn't recognize.

"Stay here," she whispered. "Focus on your magic." Then she set out along the circle's perimeter. She stopped beside the first box and touched it. The box opened, and a figure appeared amid the smoke. The female werewolf. She advanced on Almae, but the old witch cast a quick spell and disarmed her.

Almae gestured for Thea to come over. Thea helped the disoriented werewolf out of the circle and back where everyone else watched. Shane met them halfway.

Almae skipped the next three boxes and touched the fifth one. Once more, the box opened and a supernatural surged from the smoke. A warlock. I was surprised by this. I didn't think there would be a warlock inside one of the boxes ... This time, the warlock wasn't docile. He went for Almae, but before he could touch her, Drake zoomed to him and held him back.

"Hey! We're here to help," Drake said, holding the warlock's shoulders. "We've rescued you. You're confused, but I'll explain everything."

The warlock looked around, eyes wild, but finally seemed to relax a little. He followed Drake as they too retreated from the circle and joined the crowd behind us.

I tried to keep my focus on the magic, the circle.

Almae came back between Keeran and me. "Now, we finish this," she said, taking our hands. Her magic, raw and potent, flooded around us. I sent out mine to match hers, and Keeran did the same.

The magic swept across the circle, twirling around it, and pushed against the boxes. The boxes shook and melted. I gasped but didn't break my focus. Instead, I sent any magic I could spare into the spell. These boxes needed to be gone now!

In a few seconds, the six of the seven boxes were a black, bubbling goo on the ground. Almae blew a breath and the goo bubbled into oblivion.

I stared, amazed. Only one box remained, and that was only because we needed it to rescue the other supernaturals trapped in them. However, now that the other boxes were gone, the spell could never be finished.

Almae exhaled, relieved. "It's done." She wrapped an arm around Keeran's waist and another around my shoulders. "Even if another box is found, it can't be used for the spell anymore."

I opened up my senses and was so relieved I didn't feel the boxes' call. I didn't have to be afraid of being consumed by the darkness anymore.

"What now?" I asked, my voice low.

"Now, we rest," Keeran said. "Because I'm freaking tired."

Almae chuckled. Still holding on to us, she turned us around to face our friends. Thea and Shane escorted the female werewolf into the castle, Zadkiel following them. Drake and Cain tried to calm the warlock, with the rest of the princes paying attention, in case the warlock decided to be violent again.

I couldn't blame him. I remembered how Killian had reacted when I accidentally took him out of the box. After twenty years in there, anyone would go half-crazy.

Killian marched toward me. Almae dropped her arm and pushed me forward to my mate. She chuckled again as she and Keeran walked toward the castle.

Killian didn't halt before me. He slammed into me, his arms around my waist and his face in my neck. "It's over," he whispered. "I can't go back into the box anymore, you won't be lured by the darkness, and the spell will never be completed." He pulled back a little and stared at me. "We're free."

I smiled at him. "Free and together."

He matched my smile. My heart skipped a beat at his beauty. He truly should smile more. "Together, forever."

Killian leaned into me, brushing his lips on mine. I snaked my arms around his neck and held him to me, deepening the kiss. A low laugh rumbled in his chest and damn, I could get lost in him right here, right now.

KILLIAN

I spun Lavinia under my arm and pulled her to me, swaying side-to-side to the beat of the music flooding from the hidden speakers in the dining room.

Three days after we defeated the Dark Devils and destroyed the boxes, Drake and Thea threw a party for their closest friends and allies to celebrate. They didn't want to do anything formal, so we ditched the ballroom for the largest dining room in the castle, but the room seemed crowded now.

The long tables had been pushed to the sides, so they could still be used during the banquet, which had finished, but now there was a nice space to dance.

Lavinia smiled at me and my heart squeezed. Damn, she was beautiful. Tonight, she had her long hair loose and wild, with the red tips redone and bright. She wore a formal black gown that hugged her curves and made me wish we didn't have to attend parties. I wanted to keep her in my chambers—our chambers—and devour every inch of her.

"Did I tell you how pretty you look tonight?" I asked, knowing how mellow I sounded. It was all because of her.

"Dozens of times," she said, her smile widening. "But you can keep going. I don't mind."

Holy shit ... I pulled her closer until her body was flush with mine.

In the past three days, Lavinia had surprised me and the others with her control. Drake and I had tested her to see how she was doing and her score was off the charts. It was like she had been born to become a vampire, which made me extremely happy. I was so damn proud of her.

Shane appeared behind Lavinia, dancing with Lyra, a vampire female who was rising in the ranks. Yesterday, Drake had told the princes that if she kept distinguishing herself, he would have to consider adding a princess to our ranks.

I was okay with that.

Shane took Lyra for a spin and purposely bumped his shoulder on mine. "As usual, you two look like you're about to strip each other's clothes off."

Lyra laughed. "That's true."

Shane pivoted them once more so they were dancing by our side. I narrowed my eyes at him. Shane hadn't told me about his past, not yet, but I knew he had suffered a great deal. The next full moon was approaching fast and he had said he would need my help with something, though he didn't elaborate. Despite all of that, he was still the biggest charmer in this room. Lyra was his fourth or fifth dance partner of the evening. It was clear the females loved him, and even though he gave each woman all his attention when he was with her, I could clearly see he wasn't into it.

"Why don't you two do us all a favor, and go back to your room?" Shane suggested in a low voice. "And don't leave again until you can control yourselves." He winked and then twirled Lyra away from us.

I shook my head.

"You know ... they aren't wrong," Lavinia said. "We should go back to our room and ... you know, enjoy each other some more." My gut tightened. Shit, she couldn't say something like that. Not when we were in public, otherwise I would definitely rip her clothes off right here.

I cleared my dry throat. "I hear you and I agree, but what about the party? And the guests?" I glanced around.

Keeran danced with Almae while Luana talked with Thea at the edge of the dance floor. Drake was seated at the head of one of the tables, with Prince Dorian and Prince Gray beside him.

Prince Aston took demon hunter Doreen for a dance, while Prince Cain danced with his mate, the demon hunter Norah. I also saw the witch Elisa dancing with the angel Zadkiel.

The half-demons Erin and Rey were also here. They had come early and talked to Lavinia about her demon hunter side. They offered to take her to the Blackthorn Hunters Academy where she could make a Dawnblade, the demon hunter's special sword, but Lavinia refused. Her demon hunter side was weak, and with her magic unlocked and her vampire powers, she didn't need another weapon. However, she agreed to the invitation to tour the academy and the outposts, just to get to know where her father had come from, and I would be going with her.

Now, Erin and Rey talked animatedly to frost fae Farrah and werewolf Wyatt. Farrah had been after Twyla earlier, but the shadow fae had been able to avoid the other fae for most part of the day. Twyla now chatted with the angel Ariella across the room.

Aurora ran around the party, dancing here and there, jumping over chairs, or evading Mila, the young witch who was supposed to be watching over her. But everyone seemed to enjoy having her around, especially Drake and Thea. Each time they saw their child laughing and jumping, they smiled.

It was quite contagious.

"We've seen most of them for the past three days," Lavinia said. "And I don't think they would mind."

Why the hell was I fighting this? My girl wanted me and she would have me. I pressed a kiss to her throat and dragged my lips up to her ear. "Your wish is my command," I whispered.

She shivered.

I didn't care who saw us, who noticed what happened, but I held on tight to her and zipped out of the room. In three seconds, we were inside our chambers, the door banging closed behind us.

Then we slowed down.

Lavinia disentangled herself from me and took a few steps back. With a wicked gleam to her eyes and a naughty curve to her lips, she reached for the zipper of her gown.

"Come make love to me," she said, her voice sultry with desire.

My pants were so freaking tight. I advanced toward her, while working the buttons of my shirt. "You don't have to ask me twice."

Her gown and my shirt hit the floor at the same time. I wound my arms around her and leaned into her. "You have no idea how much I love you."

She clasped my shoulders, her nails sinking deliciously

into my skin. "I think I do, because it's the same as I love you."

A growl started deep into my chest. One second we were standing in the middle of the sitting room, the next we were in our bed, entangled in a way so pure, so raw, that right at this moment, it was hard to tell where she started and I ended.

Once upon a time, I didn't think happily ever after existed. Once upon a time, I would have laughed or even killed anyone who suggested I would love a witch so much.

But here we were, and I couldn't imagine anything different.

Lavinia belonged to me, and I belonged to her.

Forever.

***

Did you like Lavinia's and Killian's story? Then don't miss Shane's story—it's coming next! The first book is called *The Night Calling* and you can already pre-order it!

Don't forget to join my Facebook group, Juliana's Club, to get Evelyn and Asher's book, *The Light Witch.*

Curious about the Rite World universe? Check out this page on my website. It has the recommended reading order and links to grab more books!

THANK YOU

THANK YOU FOR READING *THE DARKEST MAGIC*!

Reviews are very important for authors. If you liked my book, please consider leaving a review on your favorite online retailer and/or on Goodreads and/or Bookbub, please!

DID YOU LIKE THIS BOOK? You can check out other books of mine:

The Midnight Test (Rite World: Lightgrove Witches 1): a clueless witch is invited to join a powerful coven—but only if she aces a difficult test.

The Demon Kiss (Rite World: Blackthorn Hunters Academy book 1): a fast-paced story about a young woman who finds out she's a demon hunter, and the half-demon intent on protecting her against all evil.

The Vampire Heir (Rite World 1: Rite of the Vampire): a dark and mysterious paranormal romance about a vampire and a young woman with a secret.

The Warlock Lord (Rite World 4: Rite of the Warlock): a

thrilling and kick-ass paranormal romance about a werewolf and warlock.

The Wolf Forsaken (Rite World 7: Rite of the Wolf): a heat-wrenching tale about a lost wolf shifter and a fae princess on the run.

Heart Seeker (The Fire Heart Chronicles book 1): an urban fantasy series about a young woman who finds herself at the center of a mysterious supernatural world.

Destiny Gift (The Everlast Series book 1): a post-apocalyptic urban fantasy series about a young woman with a special power that can save the world.

DON'T FORGET to sign up for my Newsletter to find out about new releases, cover reveals, giveaways, and more!

If you want to see exclusive teasers, help me decide on covers, read excerpts, talk about books, etc, join my reader group on Facebook: Juliana's Club!

ABOUT THE AUTHOR

While USA Today Bestselling Author Juliana Haygert dreams of being Wonder Woman, Buffy, or a blood elf shadow priest, she settles for the less exciting—but equally gratifying—life as a wife, a mother, and an author. She resides in North Carolina and spends her days writing about kick-ass heroines and the heroes who drive them crazy.

Subscribe to her mailing list to receive emails of announcement, events, and other fun stuff related to her writing and her books: www.bit.ly/JuHNL

For more information:
www.julianahaygert.com

facebook.com/julianahaygert

twitter.com/julianahaygert

instagram.com/juliana.haygert

goodreads.com/juliana_haygert

pinterest.com/julianahaygert

bookbub.com/authors/juliana-haygert

youtube.com/julianahaygert

patreon.com/julianahaygert

ALSO BY JULIANA HAYGERT

To find links and more info, go to:

www.julianahaygert.com/books/

Shorts

Into the Darkest Fire

Standalones

Daughter of Darkness

Rite World: Night Wolves

The Night Calling (Book 1)

Rite World: Vampire Wars

The Darkest Vampire (Book 1)

The Darkest Witch (Book 2)

The Darkest Magic (Book 3)

Rite World: Lightgrove Witches

The Midnight Test (Book 1)

The Midnight Spell (Book 2)

The Midnight Flame (Book 3)

Rite World: Blackthorn Hunters Academy

The Demon Kiss (Book 1)

The Hunter Secret (Book 2)

The Soul Bond (Book 3)

The Shadow Trials (Book 4)

The Infernal Curse (Book 5)

Rite World

The Vampire Heir (Book 1)

The Witch Queen (Book 2)

The Immortal Vow (Book 3)

The Warlock Lord (Book 4)

The Wolf Consort (Book 5)

The Crystal Rose (Book 6)

The Wolf Forsaken (Book 7)

The Fae Bound (Book 8)

The Blood Pact (Book 9)

The Wyth Courts

Winter King (Book 1)

Spring Warrior (Book 2)

Summer Prince (Book 3)

Autumn Rebel (Book 4)

The Fire Heart Chronicles

Heart Seeker (Book 1)

Flame Caster (Book 2)

Earth Shaker (Book 2.5)

Sorrow Bringer (Book 3)

Soul Wanderer (Book 4)

Fate Summoner (Book 5)

War Maiden (Book 6)

The Everlast Series

Destiny Gift (Book 1)

Soul Oath (Book 2)

Cup of Life (Book 3)

Everlasting Circle (Book 4)

Willow Harbor Series

Hunter's Revenge (Book 3)

Siren's Song (Book 5)

Breaking Series

Breaking Free (Book 1)

Breaking Away (Book 2)

Breaking Through (Book 3)

Breaking Down (Book 4)

www.ingramcontent.com/pod-product-compliance
Lightning Source LLC
Chambersburg PA
CBHW030629190726
48286CB00008B/2452